Changeling Press. LLC

ChangelingPress.com

Changeling MC Chapters
A Changeling Press MC Romance Sampler

Harley Wylde
Marteeka Karland
Jamie Targaet
Jessica Coulter Smith
AK Nevermore
Dana Cask

Changeling MC Chapters
A Changeling Press MC Romance Sampler
Harley Wylde, Marteeka Karland, Jamie Targaet, Jessica Coulter Smith, AK Nevermore, Dana Cask

ISBN: 978-1-60521-796-3

Publisher:
Changeling Press LLC
315 N. Centre St.
Martinsburg, WV 25404
ChangelingPress.com

Printed in the U.S.A.

Anthology Editor: Margaret Riley
Cover Artist: Marteeka Karland

The individual stories in this anthology have been previously released in E-Book format.

Table of Contents

Venom (Dixie Reapers MC 1)
A Dixie Reapers MC Romance
Harley Wylde

Ridley: I might live in a mansion in South Florida, but my daddy was a biker, and I was definitely Daddy's girl. When I found out my mom and stepdad had something horrible planned for me, I ran. Straight to the Dixie Reapers, the only place I'd ever thought of as home, but it wasn't my daddy's arms I ended up in. Venom is dark and seductive, the type of man who doesn't take shit from anyone. Despite his hard exterior, being with him makes me feel safe, and his kisses make me ache for so much more. I've never been with a man before, but even as inexperienced as I am, I know that being with Venom will ruin me for anyone else, and I don't care. I want him -- all of him -- and damn the consequences.

Venom: I hadn't risen to the rank of VP of the Dixie Reapers MC without getting my hands dirty. I'd been deep in blood and dirty money for over twenty years, could have any pussy I wanted whenever I wanted and how the fuck ever I wanted. But when an angel I hadn't seen in fourteen years came back into my life, all it took was one look in her eyes, and I was a goner. As a kid, Ridley had been this little blonde cherub who lit up the place. Now she's older, has curves in all the right fucking places, and damn if I don't want her. The fact she was the nineteen-year-old daughter of a patched member meant I needed to keep my hands to myself, and I might have, if she hadn't begged me so sweetly. Now she's mine, and I'll do anything to keep her safe, even if it means starting a war.

Prologue

Fourteen Years Ago
Venom

The little girl with the blonde curls had to be the most beautiful thing I'd ever seen. Her angelic smile could even warm my cold-ass heart. It was still a mystery to me how someone like Bull could have created a kid like that. Hell, I couldn't even imagine a woman pretty enough to make that child even existing. She was like a little china doll and had wrapped every one of my MC brothers around her little finger. Me included.

At the age of twenty-five, I'd never thought about having kids. Honestly, just the thought of knocking up one of the club sluts was enough to keep my dick from getting hard. Easy pussy could be had anytime I wanted it, but accepting my brothers' sloppy seconds, thirds, or tenths, hadn't appealed to me since my days as a Prospect. Oh, I got my dick wet, but I was a little more discerning about where I stuck it.

The gorgeous angel, all of five years old, turned that winning smile my way, and I felt myself melt. Yeah, she was going to be a heartbreaker when she got bigger, that was for damn sure. And she'd have an entire MC ready to go to battle for her. Bull almost seemed sad when he looked at his daughter, and I couldn't figure out why. The child's mom was a raging bitch, but last I'd heard, the courts had granted Bull every other weekend with the girl. We'd had a family day at the clubhouse every Saturday that Bull had his daughter, just so she could hang out with everyone. Which meant no club sluts allowed.

When her mom came to pick her up, Bull seemed to hug the girl a little tighter than usual. The blonde angel waved and smiled at everyone as her mother practically dragged her out of the clubhouse. The old ladies in the corner gave a disapproving stare, but they kept their mouths shut. No one wanted to cause problems for Bull, not when he'd fought so hard to get to see his child at all. Judges didn't look too kindly on outlaws, and Bull had spent some time behind bars, more than once.

Bull lumbered over and sat heavily on the barstool next to me. Waving to a Prospect behind the counter, he ordered a bottle of Jack, looking like the weight of the world was on his shoulders.

"What the fuck, man?" I asked. "You just got to see that gorgeous girl of yours."

"It's bad, man," Bull said. "I've loved that little girl since the moment she was born. Other than the MC, she's the only bright spot I've got."

"And you'll see her again in a few weeks."

Bull shook his head. "This was my last visit with Ridley."

"What the fuck?"

"Her mom's getting remarried. Found some rich guy in South Florida. Guy has a fucking mansion and a yacht. They're moving tomorrow. I have permission to fly down there and see her twice a year for a week each stay, but because of her age, the courts agreed that it would be best if Ridley didn't travel here unless her mom was with her. And we know that's never going to happen."

I let his words sink in, and I glanced at the door where Ridley had disappeared just moments before. It didn't seem right, separating a kid from her dad. I firmed my jaw and stared at him.

"So that's it? You're giving up?" I asked.

"What am I supposed to do?"

"Get your ass to Florida twice a year to see your kid." *Dumbass.*

Bull sighed. "Yeah. I can do that, but she's growing up so damn fast. What if she forgets about me? Her new stepdaddy is all kinds of rich and can give her everything I can't. What if she doesn't want me anymore? I'm just some broke-ass biker who drinks and swears too fucking much."

"Man, I don't care how loaded the guy is. You're always going to be her Pop. That little girl loves the shit out of you, and she always will. Ridley's too smart to let money fuck up her life. She might be five, but she's smarter than most kids twice her age. Hell, she's probably smarter than her bitch-ass mother."

"Yeah." Bull laughed. "You might be right about that. She's certainly smarter than me. Man, I don't know how I got so lucky to have such a perfect little girl. You're right, though. I'm going to see her every time I'm allowed, and I will call her every fucking day to tell her how much I love her."

I clapped Bull on the back and stood up. "One day Ridley will be all grown up and she'll be able to make her own decisions. Until then, you do what you can to make sure she knows she'll always be your number one girl."

"Thanks, Venom. You're a good kid."

I snorted. *Kid.* Hell, Bull was only ten years older than me. Grabbing my keys out of my pocket, I strolled out to my bike. I could feel the energy pulsing inside me and knew I needed a wild ride to calm me down. And if that didn't work, then I'd find a willing woman and work it off that way. My favorite bar on the other side of town was calling my name. The liquor flowed like honey, and the women were fine as hell. And I planned to enjoy both tonight.

Chapter One

I'd been looking forward to my nineteenth birthday for the past year. Nothing overly special about that number, but it meant I was finally free of this hell. I'd been convinced to stick around one more year when I'd turned eighteen, even though I'd had every intention of running straight to my daddy. But after what my mother said, I wasn't sure my dad would want me, and I had nowhere else to go. She'd talked me out of college, and against my better judgment, I'd let her. I don't know why. Maybe it was some misguided feeling that maybe, just maybe, she really loved me and everything would work out.

My mother had married Richard Benton III, a man more than twice her age, when I was five years old. He'd never had kids, and at first he treated me well. Then Mom had gotten pregnant when I was nine, and an heir had been born. I couldn't blame the kid for my problems, not really. He was innocent in all this. Well, mostly. At the age of ten, he was already something of a snot, but I knew it was because his daddy gave him everything he ever wanted.

Mom had knocked on my door an hour ago and told me to shower and put on the dress she'd hung on the back of my closet door. I'd argued, reminding her I had plans with my friends, but she'd waved me off and said this was more important. Little did she realize those plans were actually a large backpack full of clothes hidden in my car, along with a pair of boots, and a full tank of gas. I'd planned to hit the road and go home where I belonged, with the Dixie Reapers MC. But it seemed Richard had someone coming to dinner, and we would be spending the night at home as a *family*. I was fuming mad, but experience taught me it was better to do as they said. If Dad knew half the shit my mom had put me through, he'd have broken her damn neck, and sometimes I thought about telling him. All I had to do was get through dinner, then I could get the hell out of this place for the last time. I hadn't told Dad I was coming, but I hoped he'd welcome me. I knew Mom had turned him away when he'd last visited, and he was probably angry, maybe even angrier that I hadn't reached out since then. But I was his little girl, and I was hoping that still meant something to him. Even if I had screwed up.

I was showered, shaved, and dressed in the cocktail dress Mom had left, which molded to my curves and was a little shorter than I liked. My makeup was done to perfection, and my hair was curling down my back. I had to admit I looked good, and more grown-up than ever before. Stepping into my kitten heels, I heard the doorbell ring and made my way downstairs. If I made them wait, I would be punished. Not in front of guests, of course. They'd wait until their company left, and then all hell would break loose. And I couldn't afford to let that happen if I planned to escape tonight. I had planned everything as best I could, without drawing too much attention to myself, even going so far as to purchase clothes more suited to life in an MC than the mansion that horrified me. I couldn't go overboard, though, because Mom and the stepass watched my account activity, since they were the ones putting money into it in the first place.

A man in an impeccable suit stood in the foyer. His hair, more salt than pepper, was slicked back and shone under the lights. The smile plastered on his face was oily, the type you'd find on politicians and used car salesmen. But the coldness of his dark gaze made me wish I'd defied Mom after all. He studied me as I descended the staircase, his gaze caressing every inch of my body as if he were undressing me. A chill skated down my spine, and my steps faltered.

My stepdad smiled brightly when he saw me. "Ridley, come meet our guest. This is Fernando Montoya. A business associate of mine."

I made my way down the rest of the steps and stopped beside my mother and stepdad. I looked at Mr. Montoya and couldn't help but think something was very wrong. For one, where was my little brother? If this was a family dinner, shouldn't he have been invited too? For another, I'd seen men like this one before. Even my father, who was as badass as they came, didn't have the cold stare this man did, and I had no doubt there was blood on my dad's hands.

For the first time in my life, I knew true fear. I didn't yet understand what was going on, but I didn't like it.

"You're being rude to our guest, Ridley. Say hello."

"Hello, Mr. Montoya."

"Ridley." His smile chilled me.

"Well," my mother said brightly. "I believe dinner is ready. Shall we go to the dining room? Cook has prepared lobster bisque, crab cakes, shrimp scampi, and almond encrusted tilapia. And she has something very special planned for dessert."

The smirk on my stepdad's face was another clue that something wasn't right. Somehow, I had to get myself out of this situation, and I needed to do it fast. Every alarm in my body was screaming for me to bolt and not to stop running until I reached the Dixie Reapers compound. My mom and stepdad might have money, but even they wouldn't darken that doorstep. Not uninvited anyway, and no way in hell were they ever getting that invitation.

Dad had made it no secret that if Mom and Richard were to suddenly drop dead, he'd dance at the funeral and piss on their graves. Especially after his last arrest. Mom had made sure all his visitation rights were revoked, and I hadn't seen my old man in over two years. We'd still talked... at first, but it wasn't the same.

He came to the house when I turned eighteen, but I hadn't been allowed to see him. He'd kicked up a fuss until the police came to escort him away. What had hurt the most was Mom telling him that I didn't want anything to do with a dirty biker like him. I hoped like hell he hadn't believed her. The phone calls from him had stopped right after that, and I hadn't had the courage to pick up the phone and call him.

We trailed after my mother. I took the seat beside her, like I always did, and Mr. Montoya sat on Richard's other side. But the looks he kept casting my way made me uneasy. Mom noticed the attention the older man was giving me and gave another one of those falsely bright smiles. "Ridley, why don't you go sit next to Mr. Montoya. I'm sure he'd love the company after such a long journey."

I tried to hide the fact I was quaking in my fashionable heels as I moved around the table. Mr. Montoya stood and pulled out my chair. As he pushed it back after I sat down, he caressed my bare shoulders. Revulsion rolled through me, and I felt like I'd been touched by Death himself. He reclaimed his seat and began a conversation with my stepdad, but all throughout the meal, his hand wandered to inappropriate places under the table. When he shoved his hand up my dress, shoved my panties aside and stroked my pussy, I bolted out of my chair so fast it tipped over.

"S-sorry," I stammered. "Bathroom."

Without waiting to be excused, I ran from the room. My heart thundered in my chest as I locked myself in the bathroom off the foyer. The air duct over my head had always carried sounds from the dining room, and I listened in horror as my stepdad and Mr. Montoya discussed me like I was cattle.

"She'll do," Mr. Montoya said. "I'll have fun breaking her in. Once she's been properly trained, I'm sure she'll fetch top dollar."

My stomach pitched, and I nearly threw up.

"Of course, I'd prefer to see all the merchandise before paying our agreed upon price," Mr. Montoya said. "After dinner, I'll see exactly what I'm paying for and maybe take her for a test drive."

"Whatever you need," my mom said. "This deal is very important to us."

Holy shit! My own mother was *selling* me? Shit like this just didn't happen. Not to girls like me. Yeah, sure, you heard on the news about women being sold overseas to brothels, but to have it brought to own my front door... My hand shook as I slowly turned the knob and let myself out of the bathroom. I removed my heels so I wouldn't make a sound.

Marta, the housekeeper we'd had since I first moved here, was quietly standing near the front door, out of sight of the dining room. With a quick glance toward the door that led to where my fate awaited, I dashed to Marta's side. She handed me my purse and car keys.

"Be safe," she whispered. "Go straight to your father."

"Marta, I…"

She shushed me and gave me a tight hug. "I love you like you were my own. I won't stand by and let this happen to you. Now go, before they realize you're not coming back."

"Thank you," I said fervently, then soundlessly opened the front door and made my escape.

My car, a Mercedes Richard and Mom had bought on my sixteenth birthday, was parked around the side of the house. The engine was quiet, and if I kept my headlights off, no one would even know I was leaving. I slipped behind the wheel and tossed my purse and shoes on the passenger seat. Fastening my seatbelt, I shut the door as softly as I could and started the engine.

The car crept around the fountain and down the driveway. The gate was still open from when Mr. Montoya had arrived, and I breathed a sigh of relief. Once my tires touched the road, I flicked on my headlights and headed for the highway. It was a long-ass drive to Alabama, but except for gas, I wasn't fucking stopping until I saw my daddy. Mom might have done her best to separate us, but I would always be Daddy's little girl.

When I'd been on the road for hours, my stomach began to cramp from hunger and my car was almost on empty. I pulled into a small town somewhere in North Florida. After filling my tank, I left the car parked at the gas station and walked across the street to a diner. But what I saw when I stepped through the doors froze me in my tracks. My face was plastered across the TV with a ticker running underneath. *Ridley Johnson is reported as being unstable. If seen, contact the police immediately.*

I tried to pull my hair forward as much as

possible to hide my face and claimed a spot at the back of the diner, where the lighting wasn't so great. My hands fumbled with my purse, and I quietly counted what was left of my cash. I'd seen enough crime shows to know my credit cards could be traced, so I'd paid cash at the gas station and I'd pay cash for my meal. An older waitress came over, looking dead on her feet.

"What can I get you, doll?"

"A burger and fries with a sweet tea."

She nodded and scribbled my order down, not even looking at my face. As she moved away to place my order with the kitchen, some of the tension eased from my shoulders. The place was nearly empty, but I had a close call when a sheriff's deputy stepped inside. I sat frozen, scared to even breathe, until he picked up his to-go order and went back out to his cruiser.

My meal arrived a few minutes later, and I ate quickly, leaving enough money on the table to cover the bill and a tip. Gathering my purse, I headed back to my car, every nerve in my body on alert for any kind of trouble. I hit the road again and didn't stop until I'd cleared the panhandle. The nest town I stopped in was shabby, the sidewalks cracked, and the buildings crumbling. I stuck out like a sore thumb, but it was time to change. I stopped to top off my tank at a gas station that was well lit, just in case I got stuck with the car a while longer, and grabbed my backpack from the trunk. In case my family had gotten nosy, I'd hidden it in the spare tire compartment, which meant if I had a flat I was shit out of luck because both the tire and my bag and boots hadn't fit.

After filling up the car, I stepped into the grimy bathroom and stripped out of my dress and heels. I washed my face in the sink with the harsh soap provided in the dispenser and blotted it dry with the stiffest damn paper towels I'd ever touched. Pulling an elastic from my bag, I pulled my hair up into a ponytail, the long curling mass falling down the center of my back. After I had shimmied into a pair of tight, ripped jeans and put on a black tee with teal swirls and white skulls across the front, I slipped on some socks and the biker boots I'd picked up at a Harley Davidson store.

A smile flashed across my face as I studied my reflection in the cracked mirror. Aside from the golden curls, I didn't even look like Ridley Johnson anymore. At least, not the Ridley Johnson Mom had molded me to be. I hated that girl and never wanted to be her again. I stuffed my dress and heels in the trash, picked up my bag, and went back out to my car. The guy behind the counter didn't even look up from his magazine.

Now I just had one more problem. The damn car. There was no way my stepdad had put out that bulletin on me without also telling the cops what I was driving. It was a fucking miracle no one had pulled me over yet. I knew what I was about to do was risky as hell, but so was driving around in this damn Mercedes for another minute.

I'd hung around my dad long enough to know what I was searching for. Our visits might have been few, but he'd always made them count. Mom thought we were taking drives to the park or the beach, but he'd been teaching me about his way of life, and introducing me to some people she wouldn't have approved of.

I pulled up to a garage on a darkened street corner. A light inside told me someone was around, even if the place wasn't officially open. My palms were sweating again but I blew out a breath and braced myself. It was time to put the socialite behind me and be every inch my father's daughter. I pulled the keys from the ignition and boldly walked inside.

"You can't be here, bitch," a voice said harshly from deep inside.

"I need to make a trade," I said.

A man with a leather cut strolled out of the garage, the lighting just good enough that I could read *Devil's Boneyard MC -- V.P. -- Scratch.*

I had no fucking clue if it was a rival club of Dixie Reapers or not and knew I needed to tread carefully. We studied one another, his gaze taking me in from head to toe. Not in an *I want to fuck her* kind of way, more like he was assessing if I was a threat.

"I have a problem," I said. "I have a hot car and need someone to take it off my hands. All I need in return is something that will run well enough for me to get a few states away."

Scratch rubbed his jaw and looked beyond me to the silver Mercedes.

"If you change out the VIN or strip it for parts, you can make a decent amount off it," I said. "I don't care what piece of shit you give me in return as long as it gets me where I'm going. I need reliable, not flashy."

He took in my appearance again. "You know how to ride?"

His question momentarily startled me. "Ride?"

He tipped his head and sauntered back inside the garage. Against my better judgment, I followed. There was an older motorcycle sitting off to the side. The pewter gray tank and fenders had seen better days, but as I circled the bike I saw that it was in pretty decent condition. The Harley emblem, though tarnished, was a welcome surprise. I wasn't a bike expert by any means, even though Dad had tried, but I thought it was a Harley Soft Tail, which meant it would be light enough for a woman like me to handle. Unlike the big monster my dad rode.

"How well does it run?" I asked.

Scratch walked over to a wall and pulled down a key, tossing it to me. I snatched it midair, straddled the bike and turned the key. Pulling out the choke, I pressed the start button and twisted the throttle. The engine rumbled, and I let it warm up for a few minutes before slowly feathering the choke back.

A smile spread across my face. God, I'd fucking missed that sound. The thrum of the bike between my legs made me feel like I was coming home. Dad had taught me to ride when I was fourteen, and he'd rented a bike for me every time he'd visited after that, even if I hadn't been exactly been legal to drive the first few years.

"Even trade?" I asked.

The gaze Scratch gave me said he saw more than I liked, but he nodded.

"I just need to get my stuff from the Mercedes. It's unlocked," I said, handing him the car keys.

When I returned with my backpack strapped to me, my purse stuffed inside, he held out some papers to me. I glanced at them and saw it was everything I'd need to make the bike legal when I got to where I was going.

"I don't know who you belong to, baby girl, or what you're running from, but you don't fucking stop until you reach your man."

"You know who I am," I said softly.

"Picture's been all over the news tonight, statewide from what I hear. You don't appear all that unstable to me, but that family you're leaving… they're bad news. Richard Benton III is not a nice man."

"You know my stepdad?" I asked without thinking.

"Know of him. My crew won't have anything to do with the shit he's mixed up in."

I straddled the bike again and nodded.

"Who taught you to ride? Socialites like you don't know shit about bikes."

"I'm not a socialite. I'm a biker's daughter." And that was as much as I was going to tell him.

"You better run to Daddy, then, girl, because you have no idea the kind of trouble that's following you. I'll make that car of yours disappear. You been using credit cards?" Scratch asked.

"No. Cash only. I'm running low, but I think I can make it where I'm going."

"What about a phone?"

I hesitated. "Yeah, I have my cell phone."

Scratch held out his hand. "Trust me, baby girl. You don't want to keep that phone on you. Especially if Richard Benton III paid for it. They'll find you in no time."

Unease filled me, and I wondered if my stepdad had been tracking me all this time. Were the cops just moments away from coming to get me? I swung my backpack in front of me and unzipped it, removing my phone from my purse. I gave it to Scratch, and he pulled out the SIM card and battery before stomping the shit out of my phone and busting it to pieces. "Get going, girl, and like I said, don't fucking stop."

"Thank you," I said softly. Revving the engine of the old Harley, I eased out of the garage and took off down the street. It wasn't long before I was flying on the highway and crossing the Alabama state line.

By the time I'd reached the Dixie Reapers compound, I ached from head to toe and felt near to collapsing. I'd been on the road for about ten hours, and the sky was already starting to lighten. My bike came to a stop outside the gates, and a Prospect sauntered forward.

"You lost, sweet thing?" he asked, flashing crooked teeth through the beginnings of a beard.

"Get Bull."

The man rocked back on his heels. "Bull's busy."

"He's not too busy to see me."

"Sure." He chuckled. "The man's balls deep in pussy, but I'm sure he'll just run right out here to see you."

I turned off the engine, swung my leg over the seat, and stalked forward, poking the asshole in the chest and giving him the fiercest look I could muster. My shoulders were thrown back, and I hoped I looked more intimidating than I was. "Look here, you piece of shit. You get Bull, and you fucking get him now."

The man grabbed my hand and twisted so that I went down on my knee, my arm behind me at an odd angle. "I don't care who the fuck you think you are, bitch. You don't fucking touch me unless you're going to wrap your lips around my cock."

Booted steps drew near. "Is there a problem, Pete?"

"Just some fucking whore who insists on seeing Bull," the man said, twisting my arm a little more and making me cry out. "Fucking poked my chest and bowed up at me like she's fucking someone."

The man in the shadows chuckled. "Is that so?"

The boots came closer, and a dark head of hair appeared. The eyes that fastened on mine nearly took my breath away. I'd recognize those green eyes anywhere.

"Venom," I said softly.

His gaze narrowed. "Just who the fuck are you, sweetheart? Because I sure as hell don't remember you."

"I'm Ridley Johnson," I said, my voice almost a whisper as dots swam in front of my vision. If the Prospect turned my arm any more, it would break.

Surprise flashed in Venom's eyes, and he shot up to his full height. The crack of a fist filled the silence, and I was suddenly released. As I tumbled the rest of the way to the ground, strong arms wrapped around me.

"I've got you, baby girl," Venom murmured. "No one's going to fucking touch you again."

Venom lifted me into his arms, and I held on tight.

"Roll that bike up to the clubhouse," he barked at the Prospect.

"Who the hell is she?" the Prospect asked, his eyes burning with hate in the near darkness.

"Bull's daughter."

The Prospect's eyes widened, and he had that *I'm so fucked* look on his face.

The clubhouse was noisy, the air thick with smoke. Venom strode through the crowd, everyone looking at me in curiosity. He carried me down the hall and stopped at a door with his name on it. Somehow juggling me, he managed to pull out some keys from his pocket and unlocked it before stepping inside and kicking the door shut.

Venom eased me down onto a chair beside the bed and hunkered down in front of me. His gaze scanned my face and the rest of me, fury brewing in his gorgeous eyes when he saw the red marks on my arm from the Prospect.

"You wait here. I'm going to go get your daddy."

Without another word, he turned and stormed out of the room. As I slumped in the chair, I wondered if I'd made the right choice. I hadn't seen my daddy in so damn long. What if he wasn't happy to see me?

Bad Boys Multiverse
A Bad Boy Romance
Dixie Reapers MC
Devil's Boneyard MC
Hades Abyss MC
Devil's Fury MC
Bryson Corners
Owned by the Mob
Reckless Kings MC
Devoted Guardians MC
Savage Raptors MC
Devil's Boneyard MC Audio
Dixie Reapers MC Print
Dixie Reapers MC Audio
Hades Abyss MC Audio

Harley Wylde

Harley Wylde is an accomplished author known for her captivating MC Romances. With an unwavering commitment to sensual storytelling, Wylde immerses her readers in an exciting world of fierce men and irresistible women. Her works exude passion, danger, and gritty realism, while still managing to end on a satisfying note each time.

When not crafting her tales, Wylde spends her time brainstorming new plotlines, indulging in a hot cup of Starbucks, or delving into a good book. She has a particular affinity for supernatural horror literature and movies. Visit Wylde's website to learn more about her works and upcoming events, and don't forget to sign up for her newsletter to receive exclusive discounts and other exciting perks.

Harley Wylde at Changeling Press:
changelingpress.com/harley-wylde-a-196

Rocket (Grim Road MC 1)
A Bones MC Romance
Marteeka Karland

Rocket: My life pretty much took a hard left a year ago when I first met Lemon. She's wise beyond her years and as abrasive and sarcastic as they come. The second she busts my VP's balls -- literally -- I know I'd never be able to forget her. A year later I'm still infatuated with the vicious woman. When she runs off to charge hell with a water pistol, I'm right behind her wondering how we're gonna get out of this one alive. But I have a smile on my face and a determination to give this woman anything she wants. Even if it means some things in my club are going to have to change.

Lemon: Look. This is supposed to be all about how Rocket caught my eye and I decided I wanted him but there were obstacles and... phfffffff... Forget all that. What you need to know is when people are stupid, they need a kick in the... Crap. I'm not supposed to swear here. Grrrrr! Anyway, this is where I come in. Grim Road needs fixing. I'm not exactly qualified to do club... garbage, but Rocket? Yeah. I might have decided I'll keep him, so... I'm great at whipping people into shape. Grim Road, meet Lemon. See me, love me, MF'ers.

Rocket: Just pass me the beer and popcorn...

Prologue

Rocket

"I'm so sorry, Scarlet. But you should know, I'm so very, very proud of you. I love you."

Had I known what Claw would do next, I'd have taken him down. I can't say he didn't save me the trouble myself, but he was still my vice president. Without hesitating, even for a moment, Claw put the .45 to his temple and pulled the trigger. He'd shot it only a few minutes before, taking one of Hammer's legs off below the knee. The other man was now gagged, bound securely, and still writhing in pain. And rightly so. He'd terrorized Claw's daughter, Scarlet. But Claw had been as much at fault as Hammer in that. In a way, I suppose Claw had done what he knew had to be done and saved his brothers the trouble.

"Are you fucking kidding me right now?" Scarlet's eyes were wide with both shock and grief. Claw might have sold her out, but Scarlet hadn't known and the man was her father. Mars, her man, pulled her into his arms but she didn't turn her face away from the sight that had been her father. The powerful handgun he'd used had obliterated his head, spraying blood and brains all over the area.

While it was Scarlet I was concerned about, the small woman at her side snagged my attention. Lemon. She was younger than Scarlet in terms of years, but the woman was a force to be reckoned with. She held Scarlet's hand in solidarity and steadfastly refused to leave.

"Holy. Fuck." Lemon grimaced, obviously getting a little more than she bargained for, but she held on to Scarlet's hand like both their lives depended on it.

"Christ." I quickly stepped in front of the women to block their view of Claw. "Can't someone get the women the fuck out of here?" It went against everything I believed to have women witness violence of this nature. It was why I'd kept Talia, the daughter of my deceased best friend, away from everyone and everything to do with life in Grim Road. It was why I'd allowed Scarlet to leave when Claw had requested she do so. It went against everything I'd ever believed in to allow violence to touch any woman under my protection.

"Why? You think just because we're women we can't handle the hard shit? We're here to support Scarlet. She needs us here, so we're here. Seems like supporting each other is something Grim Road has a fucking problem with." The woman who spoke was the woman of Iron Tzars' sergeant at arms, Atlas. I'd heard she'd lost an unborn child fairly recently during a violent attack on their compound. I'd have thought this would be the last place she'd want to be. Given how pale she was, I was probably right. But she stood proudly beside Scarlet without flinching.

"Rose, honey." Atlas spoke gently to his wife. "Let's go. We can take Scarlet with us."

"Only if that's what Scarlet wants," Bellarose said. "If not, we stand by her."

As one, all the women surrounded Scarlet in a protective circle, Lemon at the front.

Lemon seemed to be directly challenging me with fire in her eyes, though she said nothing. I couldn't help but admire her courage in the face of what we had all witnessed. All of the women. But Lemon in particular. She technically wasn't even an adult, yet she stood her ground when I was certain there were men who would have backed down.

I glanced at Sting. "Are all your women like this?"

Sting just shrugged. "They've been through a lot this past year. And they are part of Iron Tzars. No wimps here."

"I'm sorry, Scarlet," I spoke softly to the young woman, never looking away from her. "You didn't deserve any of this."

"I got it anyway. Are you saying this was all about Hammer getting revenge for Claw killing my mother?"

"Looks that way, kid."

"I'm many things, Rocket, but I'm not a kid. Not anymore."

"Point taken. I never thought Claw was capable of betraying you. Or killing himself. Not like this. Every member of Grim Road has secrets they don't want anyone to know, and that was Claw's. I guess it's better this way. For what he did to keep his secret from you, I'd have had to kill him anyway." I sighed, scrubbing a hand over my face. "No one inside Grim knew Claw had killed Madina but me. I honestly hadn't realized Hammer knew until now. Had I known, I'd have overridden his approval of you leaving with that bastard."

Hammer thrashed and yelled behind his gag but no one seemed to pay him any attention. I was eager to get started on that motherfucker, but I would not do it with women in the area.

"It's done now. At least, Claw is done." Scarlet glanced over toward Hammer. "What's gonna happen to him?"

Sting laid out everything he had planned for the bastard. I tried to listen, knowing I fully intended to actively participate, but my attention was focused squarely on Lemon. She had her chin up, her hand firmly clasping Scarlet's. Her gaze flitted back and forth between Claw's body and Hammer, where he lay on a table that resembled an execution table. In a way I suppose it was. Hammer was going to die. Hard. Just not by lethal injection. Oh, no. He wasn't going to get off that easily.

The longer Sting spoke, the more satisfied Lemon's expression grew and she focused her entire being on the man tied to that table. The torture Sting described was brutal. Scarlet looked positively gleeful, almost maniacally so. Nothing I didn't deem appropriate, but I didn't want the women knowing how inhumane we were planning on being. Maybe it made me too old-fashioned for this day and age, but it's who I was. It was who my father had raised me to be.

Scarlet moved to stand over Hammer. "Sounds like you're getting ready to have a fun time. Bet you wished you'd never fucked with me now, huh?" She spat in his face before grabbing a scalpel and slicing a bit of skin off of his chest. Not a big piece, but enough she made the man scream behind his gag. Everything inside me rebelled. Not because I didn't think the bastard deserved everything she'd done, everything Sting described -- and more -- but because Scarlet should never have been led to feeling the way she obviously did. And because Lemon was a witness.

"We should go, Scarlet." Mars, Scarlet's man, looked desperate to get her out of there and back to the clubhouse.

"I can see this through, Mars. He was my nightmare. I can watch his demise."

"I know you can, honey. But maybe I can't."

Mars looked like he was trying not to flinch, but the fact was, the man was lying his ass off. He could totally watch the spectacle about to happen. He was trying to remove Scarlet from the situation in any way he could. I was sure he thought it would make him look weak in front of the men, but I knew better. It made him all the stronger because he thought he'd lose face and was still willing to do it if it was the only way to get his woman out without losing her trust in him.

"I'll stay in your place, Scarlet," Lemon volunteered. "I'll be your witness." I wanted to groan out loud. Did the woman have no sense of self-preservation? This could scar her for life! Probably already had. And that was the whole problem. She wasn't a woman. She was a girl. Seventeen, if I remembered correctly. She shouldn't even be here in the first Goddamned place.

"Not on your life." Danica, Lemon's sister, interjected. "You're coming back to the compound with me and Wylde. Right now."

Lemon, the brat, rolled her eyes. "You forgot to add 'young lady' at the end."

Danica looked ready to spank Lemon. Wylde looked like he was seconds away from a full-on belly laugh. Until Danica tilted her head up at him. Then he looked just as horrified as Danica had.

"I swear to God, Lemon," Danica bit out through gritted teeth. Then she pleaded with her sister. "Can you, for once in your life, please just do what I tell you?"

"If it were your best friend, Dani. If you were in the same position I'm in right now. Would you not see this through when your friend couldn't?" I'd bet my left testicle Lemon knew the answer to that question. She was too smart. She'd never have asked it otherwise.

"Sting can do that for her. He'll see this through." Danica stuck up her chin in a remarkable resemblance to Lemon. She didn't answer the question.

"But he's not her best friend. I am." Lemon looked like she was proud to call herself Scarlet's best friend. Loyalty, to this girl, meant everything. When she put herself solidly in someone's corner, she didn't leave.

Then I did the strangest thing. "Let her stay. I'll see to it she gets back to the clubhouse safely."

"Like hell," Wylde growled. "You couldn't keep one of your own women safe. You expect me to trust you with one of ours?" The fucking guy grated on my nerves something fierce. He seemed like a fun-loving geek, but Wylde was as deadly an enemy as ever I'd faced. And not just with his computer skills either. While I respected Wylde, I didn't appreciate his attitude. I couldn't allow him to disrespect me, but how could I reprimand him when I'd been thinking the exact same fucking thing?

"I'd never have permitted Scarlet to leave the safety of our territory if I'd known she'd be in danger. I know I have a lot to make up for because of Claw, but despite what it looks like, I take the safety of everyone in my club seriously. Especially our women and children." I should have followed up with her. It hung in the air unspoken between us like a specter.

"I'll keep an eye on them both, Wylde." Sting spoke softly, gripping Wylde's shoulder. "I'll bring her back. If she wants to stay, let her. Trust her to know where her limit is." I raised an eyebrow. Sting was a young man but apparently wiser than I was. I was with Danica on this, even if I'd said otherwise. I glanced once at Lemon. Her expression took my breath. It didn't matter what anyone said. Lemon wasn't leaving until she was Goddamned good and ready.

"Sting, I don't want her to do this. This is going to be brutal."

"I got this, Dani. Go on." Lemon actually reached out to her sister and squeezed her hand. She squared her shoulders and gave her sister a small grin. It was the first show of nerves she'd shown since immediately after Claw had shot himself.

Wylde whispered softly to Danica. I didn't hear what he said, but Danica didn't try to insist Lemon leave with her. Wylde guided her gently out of the barn. Lemon moved next to Hammer where he lay on the table. The men from Iron Tzars had started IVs on the guy and he now had one in the bend of his elbow and in the side of his neck. Both had fluids dripping slowly, but steadily through them.

"Looks like we're gonna be here a while, Hammer." Lemon grinned down at him. "I'm new to this whole death by torture bit, but I'm confident I can outlast you."

Just like that, I fell in love. I knew beyond any shadow of a doubt Lemon would be mine. Not today. Not until she was legal and I could be sure she was ready. But this woman would be my old lady. And I would rule her. The fun would be in the taming. It would possibly take a lifetime. But by fucking God, we'd have a blissful time of it.

Chapter One

Rocket

The heavy air in the compound's meeting room hung like a shroud, thick with exhaust and the sharp tang of spilled beer. I stood at the head of the long table, my gaze sweeping over the assembled brothers of Grim Road.

"All right, listen up," I called out, my voice rough as gravel. The room fell silent, every pair of eyes locked on me, waiting. "For those of you who don't know, Claw and Hammer are gone." More than one of the brothers raised an eyebrow, glancing at the man next to him. I'd taken eight of my most trusted men but hadn't called on the entirety of Grim Road. Mainly because I knew in my heart Scarlet wasn't being held against her will by Iron Tzars. As a rule, the men in Grim were a pretty Goddamned secretive lot, so when I'd called on my officers to ride with me, they'd simply done as I'd asked and hadn't said a fucking word to anyone else in the club.

"The fuck?" Spike had been leaning casually against a table, his arms crossed over his chest. He stood up straight, looking around at the others. Spike was also a close friend of Hammer. They'd served together both in and out of the Marines. "What do you mean gone?"

"Dead." I didn't mince words. They all needed to know because that left the VP position open and I needed to really think about who I put there.

There had always been cliques in the club. Men who trusted some more than others. We were all so used to operating by ourselves or in groups of two or three that thinking and operating as a group had never been something we'd adapted to. Grim Road had been around for a long time and hadn't always worked like this, but as the political environment changed over the decades and the old guard ushered in the new, we'd... changed. It wasn't that we didn't trust each other, but we... didn't really trust each other. Exactly.

"What happened?" Bear finally broke the silence weighing down the room. I knew he would be the one to speak for the group. His voice was a soft growl. The man could be demanding without being overly aggressive. His demeanor had always been a direct contrast to my own. Sometimes, he could balance me with the rest of the club without even trying. I was pretty sure he'd be the best choice for a VP. But not just yet. I needed to straighten out this fucking mess before I made any permanent changes in the club.

"There's a lot several of you guys don't know and I ain't tellin'. Not my story. But Claw put Scarlet in the hands of a sadistic bastard, and she was hurt because of it."

"Wait." Mace held up a hand. He was a man I should have taken with us. Of all the men in Grim Road, Mace was the steadiest. But he hadn't been in the compound when we'd left, having stayed behind to clean up from our last mission. "Didn't Scarlet leave with Hammer?" He glanced at Crush. "From what I heard she was supposed to be Hammer's old lady when she came of age. What happened?"

"Again, it's a long story, but Hammer and Claw had... history. I thought the same as you did. That Scarlet wanted to leave with Hammer. But that wasn't the case. Once he got her out of the compound, he abused her physically and mentally. Getting even with Claw for a past incident. One I should have dealt with years ago. So part of this whole fuckin' mess is on me."

"So, they're dead." Bear gave me a hard look.

"How'd they die?"

I shrugged. "Claw blew his own brains out. Hammer... well. There were quite a few pieces of the man when we finished with him."

"We?" Dom raised an eyebrow and glared at me. Hard.

"Yeah. Me, the men I took to Evansville, Indiana, and a few members of Iron Tzars."

"You were there?" Bear looked disapproving. I frowned at him.

"Yeah. I was fuckin' there. A member of this club has to die, I'm the one doin' it. Problem?"

Bear stared at me. Hard. "Yeah. I got a fuckin' problem. You went into another club's territory with only a handful of men. You went lookin' for a war but didn't take enough to back you up." He lifted his chin. "Tell me I'm wrong."

I shook my head. "Not sayin' you are, Bear. But I won't lie. I was pretty sure Hammer was lyin' when he said Scarlet was being held by Iron Tzars against her will. I know some of those men as well as I know you."

Bear grunted. "Mars, in particular."

"Yeah. Scarlet is with Mars. He made her his old lady."

"You gonna respect his claim?" Bear always did know how to ask the hard questions. It solidified my belief he was the right man to be vice president.

"It's what Scarlet wants. Woman's been through enough without us fightin' over her like dogs over a bone."

Ringo snorted. "Well, that and the old ladies of Iron Tzars are more than a little rabid. Especially that one called Lemon. Eh, Prez?" Yeah. Ringo had my number.

"The women of Iron Tzars ain't our problem. But

Scarlet wants her sisters to come to Evansville. I think it's a good idea."

Dom shook his head. "Not sure that's a good idea. They should at least be given a choice."

"Scarlet is their only living relative. You can bet your ass Wylde has already worked some magic to make her their legal guardian. Besides, you know they think Scarlet hung the moon. They'll go wherever she is. Hell, they fought like wildcats to go with her when she left with Hammer."

"He's right." Fang's deep voice penetrated the soft murmur around our meeting room. "Those girls will want to be with Scarlet. It's not a bad idea to ask them, though. Just to be sure. The last thing we want to do is make them feel like they don't have any choices. One or both of them will bolt like a wild fuckin' bronco if we do." There were more than a few chuckles around the room. Sunshine and Rainbow weren't quite on the same level as Lemon, but they were both skirting the edge of wild.

"Agreed. Now. Have Gina tell them to get packed. I'm expecting Brick to roll in here with a contingent that includes Mars and Scarlet within the hour. They'll expect the girls to be ready, and I don't intend to be more of an ass than I've already been."

"No one expects you to cave to another club in our territory, Prez," Bear snapped. "You don't think those girls need to go, fuck the lot of 'em."

"No. This is one time I'll allow it. At least, if the girls want to go. I owe it to Scarlet. After what she went through, that woman can have any fuckin' thing she wants. She needs her sisters right now. Probably more than they need her."

Byte stood. "I'll go help Gina. She had a thing for Hammer. Think it's best if she doesn't find out about it around the girls. They'll meet you guys at the entrance to the inner compound." He was the best person for the job. Sunshine and Rainbow adored the tech wiz. Probably because he kept them in the latest gaming consoles and computers. He was right to think Gina didn't need to hear about Hammer until she was away from the others. Byte would see to it she had privacy when she was told. If anyone could keep things smooth in this instance, it would be Byte. "When Scarlet gets here to pick them up, she can ask them in front of me. I'll honor their wishes and be careful of everyone's feelings."

"Good." I looked around the room, studying each of them. "We have one more thing to get out of the way." I met the gaze of each man present, really studying them. No one hurried me. It wasn't their way. We were all trained to wait patiently, no matter the circumstances. In our line of work, there was no room for mistakes. We were each other's only backup. Sometimes we didn't even have that. Each man could hold everything inside and not give anything away. Even torture would yield few results. If any. So I had to watch everyone very carefully. I'd trusted every person in the club.

Even Hammer. Even knowing the history between him and Claw and Madina. Even knowing Claw's woman had given birth to Hammer's twins. Claw had always treated the girls like his own, but now I had to be sure the threat to them was over. Also, I needed to know who in my club could be sadistic enough to contemplate hurting our children. No matter what the reason, that was as step too fucking far. "Hammer terrorized Scarlet. Beat her and threatened to harm Sunshine and Rainbow if she retaliated or left him." A couple of the men glanced at each other, showing more of a reaction than I'd expected, but more than a few simply gazed on stoically, giving nothing away. "He told her he had someone in the club keeping an eye on the girls. That one word from him and they'd suffer. I'm paraphrasing, but I took it the same way Scarlet did. Hammer had someone in Grim Road working with him to destroy Claw through his children."

"That's fucked up," Spike muttered. "Only a fuckin' coward preys on kids to get back at an enemy."

"It's worse than that," Dom said, giving me a glance. I nodded. The club needed to know. "Sunshine and Rainbow are Hammer's daughters. Claw is the one who killed Madina."

That got more than a few disbelieving grumbles.

"No fuckin' way," Spike snapped. "Not possible."

"Which event are you referring to?" Dom asked. "Because there's a couple things I had trouble with."

"Fuckin' all of it! Hammer would never disrespect a brother by movin' in on his woman. Madina and Claw had been an item for years before Hammer even patched in."

"I confirmed the first two with Hammer myself." I scrubbed a hand over my face. "Look. I know this is a real dick punch, but the fact is the only innocent parties in all this shit are Scarlet, Sunshine, and Rainbow. Hammer fucked Claw's woman. By all accounts he loved Madina. Claw and Madina had… issues. I'm not certain what they all were, but I know Madina was unhappy. I wasn't there when she told him about the babies, but I suspect she was going to leave him."

"The signs were there." Bear stroked his beard as he mused. "I remember thinking there was something going on between the two of them, but…" He shrugged. "Not my business."

"Fuck." Spike was possibly the most transparent of all of us. His work in Black Ops usually had to do with scouting a mark and planning the strike. Even though he had the training, he wasn't as experienced with deep cover as the rest of us. "I still don't see it. Hammer would have taken revenge on Claw directly. Not by going through kids to do it."

"Think about it, Spike." Falcon gripped Spike's shoulder in an effort to calm down the other man. "Claw was the VP. Hammer was a newly patched member. How's he gonna fight Claw?" He looked up at me. "What I don't understand is how Hammer could have someone ready to harm the girls if he knew they were his."

I nodded to Falcon. "Good point. When we took Hammer apart, I got the impression he was so eaten up with hate he didn't give a fuck. Claw had raised Sunshine and Rainbow as his own. Hammer knew he'd never have their loyalty and love the way Claw did. I think he distanced himself from the fact they were his daughters. He gave away more than I thought he would, and I think that was only because of what we did."

"Every man has his breaking point." Falcon nodded like he understood. "Must have been bad."

"Was." I barely suppressed a shudder. What we'd done to Hammer... Yeah. He deserved what we did and worse, but I had no idea if I could have done it by myself. If any of us could have. The men of Iron Tzars were pretty hardened and used to torture, but Hammer had been subjected to a special kind of hell. While it made my stomach roil, I still regretted none of it. "Ain't goin' over what we did so don't ask. Like I said. He wasn't in one -- or even a few -- pieces when we finished.

"So. We have a few things to discover. First, I want a rundown of Hammer's movements, Crush. I want to know where he was every second of every day in the weeks leading up to him and Scarlet leaving. You can't find a pattern or a person of interest, go back further." I gave my intel officer a hard look. "I want everything. And I mean everything. No matter how trivial you think it is."

"Maybe Hammer was fuckin' with you." Spike spoke up again. "Maybe he just wanted you to think there was a problem in the ranks."

"Wouldn't put it past him," Falcon agreed. "He's a wily son of a bitch."

"Was." I grunted. "And I get your point. But trust me when I say he was in no shape to make that kind of story convincing. All he could do was withhold information. Which he steadfastly did. Even when he was screaming. No. he had someone prepared to make good on his threat. Probably part of the reason he wanted to leave town. It gave him free rein to hurt Scarlet while distancing himself from any violence toward the girls. At least, I hope so. If not, then he was a truly evil man. And if there's one person that evil in our midst, there could be more. We're a secretive lot by nature, so this hurts in ways we've not even considered before."

"On it, Prez," Crush said softly. "I'll get Byte to help, if you're good with that."

I thought about Byte. He was younger than Crush by close to ten years and fresh out of the CIA. He'd put in his time and that time hadn't been kind to him. He'd also been on more than one mission with Hammer. "He gonna have a problem with this? I know Byte and Hammer were close."

"They weren't." Crush snorted. "Hammer was an asshole in the extreme. Byte tolerated him because he was part of the club, but I know Byte can absolutely believe this of him. I certainly do."

"Fuckin' little pissants. Both'a you," Spike muttered.

"Spike, you're out of this meeting." I had to take a stand on this if we were going to ferret out who was working with Hammer. "Listen up, people." I put as much hard authority as I could in my voice. "I know Hammer is guilty. That's not up for debate. What I'm interested in is finding out who was working with the son of a bitch. If your loyalty is to him, you need to get the fuck out." I turned to the now fuming Spike. "You're confined to quarters until further notice. I'll have food prepared and sent up by officers I trust."

"Come the fuck on, Prez! You might have had time to process this, but I don't remember a single fuckin' thing that would lead me to believe Hammer was capable of harming a kid. Not one."

"You can process it in your quarters."

"Fuck!" Spike smacked the back of the chair, tipping it over, and stormed out of the room.

"Anyone else?"

There were a few grumbles but nothing overt. I could see Crush noting every single one of them mentally, too. Crush was the more unbiased of the two, but Byte would be fine. Crush would keep him focused on the right thing. It was the way they worked. While Byte was the better investigator, Crush could keep his personal feelings out of the work. I figured it came with age.

"Good. No one is exempt from this investigation, Crush. Even me. I want to know everyone Hammer had contact with and to what extent. I absolutely will not have anyone in this club who is willing to harm a woman in our care unless there is a fuckin' good reason, or willing to harm a child for any fuckin' reason."

"Understood." Crush shook his head slightly, closing his eyes and taking a breath. I got it. He kept an eye on things most of us would prefer to be kept quiet, but this was a whole different level of spying on his brothers. It set him apart and now he was including Byte. No one blamed Crush for what he had to do. Not really. But it was still damned uncomfortable to know he knew some of the darkest secrets some of them had. He would never mention anything to anyone else, and he only talked to me if he deemed the situation a security risk. This was something else entirely, and we all knew it. Thing was, of all of us, I trusted Crush the most. He was the only one who ever willingly came to me with issues of his own. He said if he could know everyone's private business in the club, I could know his.

"Good. You two get on it. I want a detailed report every twelve hours, or anytime you find something important." I gave the room a hard stare, daring anyone to go against me.

"Don't you think that's an invasion of privacy, Prez?" The kid, Jackhammer -- yeah, wasn't touching that one -- raised a finger in the air. He had an innocent, dumb expression on his face I would have found adorably naive and laughed it off in any other circumstance. Given the situation, though, I was less than amused.

"No. You done somethin' you don't want Crush to find out?" I raised an eyebrow.

"Well, yeah, actually. Don't we all?" There were some grunted assents and some scowls thrown the kid's way. Looked like the club was solidly divided on this one.

"Tough shit." I grinned, but knew that smile didn't reach my eyes. "He's investigating me too. And yeah. I got my own fuckin' secrets. The only people who will know everything are Crush, Byte, and me. You don't like it? You can leave." I let my mask of civility drop so everyone in the meeting could see how serious and fucking furious I was. "But rest assured. I will find out who was working with Hammer, whether he's here or not. And I will annihilate them, whether or not they're still part of this club."

Having said my piece and given my orders, I left the meeting room to go to the front gate and await the Iron Tzars contingent. And... her. Because I knew there was no way Scarlet would come back to Grim Road without Lemon. I was anxious to see how Lemon dealt with this bunch. I had a feeling fireworks were about to fly. I wouldn't interfere, but I was damned sure going to enjoy the show.

Bones MC Multiverse
Bones MC
Shadow Demons
Salvation's Bane MC
Black Reign MC
Iron Tzars MC
Grim Road MC
Bones MC Print Duets
Bones MC Audio
Salvation's Bane MC Audio
Iron Tzars MC Audio

Marteeka Karland

International bestselling author Marteeka Karland leads a double life as an action romance writer by evening and a semi-domesticated housewife by day. Known for her down-and-dirty MC romances, Marteeka takes pleasure in spinning tales of tenacious, protective heroes and spirited heroines. She staunchly advocates that every character deserves a blissful ending.

Marteeka finds joy in baking, and gardening with her husband. Make sure to visit her website to stay updated with her most recent projects. Don't forget to register for her newsletter which will pepper you with a potpourri of Teeka's beloved recipes, book suggestions, autograph events, and a plethora of interesting tidbits.

Marteeka Karland at Changeling Press:
changelingpress.com/marteeka-karland-a-39

Hero (Hounds of Hell MC 1)
A Hounds of Hell MC Romance
Jamie Targaet

Jade -- I came back to town because my grandmother passed away and she was the only family I had left. Grams never wanted me involved with the MCs, but I always knew my father was a member. That was all I knew about him. Now he's the president of Hounds of Hell MC. Or, as it turns out, he could also be the president of their rival MC, the Cottonmouths. Hounds of Hell MC sent one of their men, Hero, to keep me safe until my parentage gets figured out. No one is telling me why that's necessary. I should go back to Providence. But I'm done with grad school, and there's really nothing for me back there. And Hero is one beefy, gorgeous temptation of a biker. Part of me wants to stay here, in the home where I grew up. Part of me just wants *him*.

Hero -- When my prez gave me the babysitting assignment to keep an eye on the daughter he's never known, I resented it. Until I got a look at her. Choosing me to protect her was the right call. The Cottonmouths took her from me once. No one is taking her away from me again -- no matter who has to die. I don't care who her father is. Jade is mine.

Chapter One

Jade

"Are you sure you want to be doing this?"

Jaeden smiled at the kind older gentleman who'd been her grandmother's companion for the last couple of decades. Emery Phillips' round face was heavily lined, and he was missing a couple of teeth. But his blue eyes were bright and friendly. When he smiled? Yeah. She could totally see how he'd won the heart of one Mina Dock.

Her heart clenched in her chest thinking about the loss of Grams. The stubborn old woman had loved her to death. She'd been the only family Jade ever had. "I *could* sell it," she told Emery as they stood on the front porch where she'd played as a child. "But now that I'm done with grad school there's really no reason to stay in Providence. I think I'd like to settle here."

The old sign she'd made in school still stood in the flowerbed at the edge of the porch. "Gram's Garden," it read in faded red paint. And on the bottom step, if she looked closely, Jade could just make out the hash marks she'd made each time her grandmother had run off her estranged father through her childhood. Exactly seven marks. And those were the times she was aware of.

Okay, so not all her memories were happy. But as she grew older, she had a better idea why Grams did what she did. Her grandmother had tried to do what was best for her.

"He never stopped coming here, asking about you, you know," Emery went on. "Last time he was here was a couple of weeks before she died."

Jade blew out an exhale. "You were here?"

The older man shook his head.

Well, she was grown now and had just finished grad school. If her father stopped by, maybe she'd talk to him. Yeah, he was supposedly the leader of a notorious biker gang and she'd heard some wild stories through the years. But she wouldn't judge him based on that. "If he comes by, I'll handle it," Jade assured him.

Emery's gaze held a note of concern. "You get she didn't want you in their world, right? That she was trying to keep you away from that bunch?"

Jade nodded. She understood very well.

Her mother, Vanessa Dock, had a wild streak a mile wide according to Grams. As a young woman of nineteen, she fell in with the wrong crowd. She'd accidentally gotten pregnant once but lost it because she couldn't kick alcohol and drugs.

When she'd gotten pregnant with Jade, Grams had essentially placed her daughter on lockdown. Took her to rehab, to doctor visits. Her grandmother had taken care of her mother and helped her to turn her life around.

Gram's efforts paid off. Vanessa gave birth and took care of Jade. She got a job and had plans to get back to school. The three of them lived there in the home she'd inherited. They'd been happy judging by all the pictures. She just wished she could remember more.

Her mother's death in a car accident when Jade was three years old was a cruel irony.

"He tried hard to take you away from her once your mother passed," Emery explained. "Wasn't above threatening her either. Just watch yourself with them. Nothing but bad news."

Jade's confidence in talking to her father waned a little at the warning. Emery ran a bar on the outskirts of town and knew most of the locals, most especially the MCs. Was there something he wasn't telling her?

"I will," she told him, knowing he was looking out for her. "Thank you."

Emery helped her carry the few items she'd brought with her into the house. It wasn't much. The funeral was tomorrow. She had a lot to do between settling her grandmother's affairs, going through the house, and moving everything from her apartment in Providence.

She'd just finished her graduate degree in the summer session. She could participate in the fall commencement at the university back in Rhode Island, but she doubted she would. Not now. The job as research assistant ended last week, and she had a couple of weeks left on her lease to get everything moved and say her goodbyes.

They talked for a while before Emery headed back home, telling her he'd pick her up for the funeral tomorrow. And she was grateful for that, especially when she walked back into her childhood home alone.

Grams was gone.

She'd had a stroke in her sleep, they'd said. It had been quick. Emery had called her three nights before to let her know. It still broke Jade that she'd never gotten to say goodbye.

She talked to Grams each week on the phone. The last time had been two days before she passed. Her grandmother had sounded just the same. She'd been trying to plant her garden, putting up with Emery's nonsense as she worked. Never anything negative to speak of. Always ended the call with, "I'm so proud of you. I love you, Jade."

Jade didn't realize she'd started to cry. Sinking to the floor by her Grams' bed, she finally let the grief drop over her now that she was here. Now she was alone. All she had was a degree she didn't have immediate plans for, a couple of loser boyfriends, and the house that was now hers.

When she'd managed to pull herself off the floor, she found herself looking through her grandmother's bedside table. Most people kept junk in such drawers, but not Mina Dock.

There were her medications and an emery board. A couple of hair ties. Then there were the pictures.

She only had framed pictures of Jade and her mother on the table next to the lamp. In the drawer, in a small hand-sized photo album were other pictures. Private ones that must have been just for her. A picture of Jade as a baby on her mother's hip. Another of Mina and Emery, kissing under the mistletoe last Christmas.

Jade smiled. She'd taken that photo herself.

The final photo Jade hadn't seen before. A picture of her mother when she was younger, cuddled up on the lap of a man who looked very familiar. She couldn't help but stare at the picture. The man who held her was a large guy with thick waves of dark hair, hazel eyes, and a killer smile. He had a leather jacket with a wolf insignia of some type on it.

Jade's heart flew. Was he her father?

She'd always been too scared to really look at him when he showed up when she was little. Most of the time, Grams made her flee into the house like he wasn't even allowed to look at her. But the few times Jade hadn't been sent into the house, she didn't make eye contact. She tried not to move.

Grams told her he wasn't a good man. That always made her worry. What if he did take her away one day?

Jade always tried to make herself small,

unnoticeable. When she was a teenager, she didn't go outside as often so she didn't remember him coming by. But he must have.

Her father had apparently been so bad Grams wouldn't allow him near her. What had he done? It was the conversation they'd never had.

And why in twenty-four years had he never given up?

When he stopped by, and apparently, he would, how would that go?

Putting herself together again, Jade decided to head into town for takeout. She'd driven most of the day and really hadn't stopped to eat much of anything.

As she headed out to her SUV, she had no idea someone was in the shadowy corner of the property she'd inherited, watching her.

* * *

Hero

Christian Hammond, Hero to his brothers, watched from the inside of his Jeep as the leggy brunette made her way to the small SUV. She was probably heading to town, so he decided to give her a head start and see what she was up to. He didn't have anything else going on at the moment.

When Razor told him to go see if his daughter had come home, Hero had been annoyed by the assignment. What the fuck was he? A babysitter?

Now that he got a look at her, he didn't have much to complain about. Her jeans were tight, showing off legs a mile long and a nice ass to go with them. Her baggy college sweatshirt didn't do her any favors, but her long dark hair framed a face that was delicate, beautiful.

How the fuck did Razor have a daughter who

looked like *that*?

His club president probably wouldn't appreciate him ogling his only child the way he was either but... *Look at her.*

Scrubbing a hand over his beard, Hero waited as she started the car and threw on her seat belt. Finally, she started down the long gravel driveway that took her to Route 8. Hero let her reach town, not having any trouble spotting her as she parked on Main Street and headed straight for the local coffee shop.

Hero liked the way she walked with her shoulders back, her head held high. Confidence was sexy as hell on a woman and the sway of her round little ass didn't hurt either.

His phone rang before he could shut off the engine and follow her on foot. Not surprisingly, it was Razor.

"She make it into town?" he asked.

"Yeah," Hero told him. "Old man Phillips was there and talked to her for a while."

"Hmm." A pause. "I've got Snow working on the girl over at the attorney's office. She's sweet on him. We'll see if she can find out if my girl means to keep the house or sell it."

"Want me to stay on her?" As much as he'd bitched to himself about the assignment, he was minding a lot less now.

A long pause which was odd. Razor usually didn't have any trouble issuing orders.

"Yeah, man, I need you to," Razor said in a lower voice. "I'd give it to the prospects but... I need someone I can trust on this. I'm going to need eyes on her at all times until I can resolve some shit. If you'd stay on her until midnight, I'll have Snow come relieve you."

What was this about?

Hero wouldn't question his prez. He appreciated that Razor trusted him.

"I'm on it," Hero told him. "She's here in town now, so I'm keeping an eye out."

"Talk to you soon," Razor told him, ending the call.

His daughter had come home for the funeral just like Razor said she would.

Everyone in Mercy knew Mina Dock. The old woman had a lot of friends so tomorrow was bound to be a circus.

The girl's grandmother taught school for years and had retired not too long ago. She was apparently as stubborn as Razor and that was saying a lot. The president of his club had been trying for years to see his daughter, to see if Mina would agree to any type of shared custody arrangement or visitation rights. The old woman wouldn't hear of it.

Razor never talked about it. Hero had heard stories.

Razor had never taken an old lady, and the girl's mother, by all accounts, had been one of the club sluts for a time. Apparently, when she got knocked up, Mina Dock took control of the situation and that was the end of it.

Razor had a daughter he wasn't allowed to see any more than he had her mother before that. The girl's mother died a long time ago. Mina Dock had to have been one tough bitch to have kept Razor away.

Hero climbed out of his Jeep when she darted back out of the shop, a coffee cup in hand as she continued up the sidewalk. Her movements were fast, determined.

Hero grinned. *There it was.*

Razor walked like that when he meant business, or he was pissed at someone.

Speeding up a little, Hero headed in her direction. He was enjoying the sunny day, his curvy assignment. Things could certainly be worse.

When he saw a white delivery van come up the road behind him, he couldn't have said why he noticed. Three familiar-looking men jumped out and he froze.

Fucking Cottonmouths. What the fuck were *they* doing here? They weren't wearing their cuts but he knew who they were.

And he'd lost her. He didn't know which shop she'd darted into, but he moved even faster. He couldn't help but feel they were here for her, same as him.

Fuck.

While he was fairly sure he could handle the three of them on his own, he'd been in enough skirmishes to know better than to be one against three with the girl in play. He couldn't risk texting, so he called Razor back.

"Yeah."

"Three Cottonmouths just showed up," Hero said quickly. "We're on Main Street."

"Really?" Razor didn't sound amused. "The posse's coming."

"Thanks." Hero pocketed his phone and watched as the three of them darted across the street, walking in front of him on the sidewalk. They didn't even notice him.

The first one was Jimmy Jazz, a scrappy little fucker who put on a good show until things got physical. Then he tended to fade into the background like the little coward he was. The second one, Big Dog, had the tender sweetness of a pit bull and was one hell of a fighter. Hero knew he could stand toe-to-toe against the massive, shaggy-looking asshole. But he'd rather not.

The one that worried him was Baby Face.

Walking ahead of the other two, Baby Face was average size with a pretty face the girls loved. And he could draw them to him like a bee charmer, all honey and smiles.

His pretty face concealed a black heart. A more sadistic little fucker Hero hadn't met. What he lacked in size, he made up for in savagery. He was good with knives and could take most down with his blades before they even realized they were bleeding out.

He'd cut up many a club slut, too.

That they were here for Razor's daughter had him wondering what the hell was going on. Why were the Cottonmouths after the girl?

When she darted out of another shop - he didn't know which store it was - his heart sank to see them right on her heels. Hero sped up, hoping his backup got there fucking fast.

Baby Face called out to her. When she didn't stop, he did it again.

Don't stop.

But she did, turning to face them and her eyes widening in fear.

The van raced up then and screeched to a halt next to them. She dropped her coffee and ran. Baby Face caught her by her long dark hair, giving the other two time to snatch her off the street and quickly haul her into the back of the van.

Baby Face looked around as he climbed in himself, his gaze meeting Hero's. The bastard winked at him before slamming the van doors hard.

As Hero watched, the van sped away.

* * *

Jade

When Jade woke up, her head was pounding and her mouth was sand dry. Her vision was blurry when her eyes slit open. When she didn't recognize the room she found herself in, her heart lurched in fear. *Where was she?*

All her grandmother's warnings about MCs echoed in her mind as her eyes adjusted to the dim, dirty room with no windows. She could hear the low din of voices that didn't sound too far away.

The last thing she remembered was the three men chasing her down the sidewalk in town. It had been nothing for them to snatch her off the street and throw her in the back of their van.

When she went to sit up and fetch her phone out of her jeans pocket, she found her right wrist was hand-cuffed to the dirty cot she'd been lying on.

Why am I handcuffed? What do they want with me?

How long had she been there? Her grandmother's funeral...

She had to find a way out. Trying to stay calm as fear crept into her mind, she scanned the room around her. An old metal desk was shoved in one corner. Papers, books, old coffee cups, and assorted items were scattered all over it. Nearby was an office chair that had seen better days.

Old calendars hung on the wall, some with lewd photos of scantily clad girls. Others had photos of vintage motorcycles. All of them faded, some with stains. The most recent year was 2013 best she could make out.

The back of her head really hurt. With her free

hand, she found a lump at the back of her skull, a scab on her scalp. When she reached for her jeans pocket, she found her phone was gone. As her mind scrambled for answers, the door to the shabby little room opened. The young man who walked in wore a denim cut with a black shirt and jeans. She recognized him as one of them who'd taken her. Of course he was a biker.

In another world, she might have considered him handsome. He had blue eyes and a face any actor would beg for, all sharp cheekbones and a jawline for days. Rich locks of chestnut hair framed that face, and his smile was stunning when he turned it on her.

The smile didn't reach his eyes.

Before he could speak, two more bikers came in behind him, pushing her anxiety higher. One was tall and lanky with spiky brown hair. One was huge with shaggy hair and a scary, bearded face.

"Our friend is awake," the pretty one told them, his gaze cold on her.

"What are we going to do with her?" the shaggy one asked. "The Hounds are going to be on our ass."

The Hounds? An image of the wolf on the cut the man wore in the old picture of her mother flashed in her mind.

"Sure they are." His blue-eyed gaze stayed on her unnervingly. "Razor's always thought she was *his* kid."

"You don't even know who Razor is, do you?" he demanded of her. "Mina kept you hidden away, didn't she? But Mina's gone. She can't save you now."

Tears stung the backs of her eyes at the mention of the only family member she had left. "What do you want with me?" Jade asked. It sounded a lot braver in her head. "I'm here for the funeral. That's all."

"I know," the pretty one told her, taking a knee

next to the cot.

He was two feet away, but she was pushing herself closer to the wall, away from him.

"Hero saw us," the biker with spiked hair warned.

Hero?

"Hero ain't going to do shit!" Color flooded the leader's face as he stared at her wide-eyed. "By the time they figure out where she is…"

"Where's that?" the shaggy one asked.

"I thought Big Billy could use another girl for his club." The leader grabbed her chin roughly in his hand, turning her face to one side before she managed to shove him away. "What do you think she'll get for a night?"

Jade stared at him in shock. *Human trafficking?* She couldn't have heard him right.

"She'll be a club slut, just like her mama was," their leader continued.

Panic rioted in her mind. Grams never talked about her mother's time with the bikers. Had her mother wronged someone? Why come after *her?*

Had her mother been a prostitute? Or had she been trafficked? Not knowing the details, combined with the terror of her current situation, had her fighting to stay silent.

"I-I don't know anything about my mother," Jade said slowly. "She died when I was little. I'm sorry if she did… something…"

"You're *sorry?*" The leader laughed then, a humorless sound. "Sorry? Sorry is what you're going to be after a few weeks on your fucking back." The leer the shaggy one cut her had her stomach turning.

"What do you think boys?" he went on. "Think we should break her in for Big Billy? Give her a preview of her new life?"

The one with spiked hair cut him a look. "Ain't she your half-sister though?"

What? Oh, God. That couldn't be true, could it?

"The fuck you say to me?"

The leader was on his feet in an instant, color flooding his angry face as he spun to face his companions. The back of his cut showed a coiled-up snake looking ready to strike. *Cottonmouth* was printed on the denim above it.

Grabbing a handful of the other man's shirt, the leader slammed him against the nearest wall hard. "She's not going to be anything but a used-up whore once she's been in Billy's a while." He got in the other man's face. "That's all your dumb ass needs to know."

The man in his clutches already had his hands up. "Sorry, Baby Face. Didn't mean nothing by it. You can do whatever."

Baby Face?

"That's right." Letting the man go, he turned to face her. His face was lit up in evil glee. "We need to get her to Billy's. Tonight."

Jade didn't like the way all three of them looked her over.

"Give her another dose," Baby Face told them. "If she's strung out, she'll be easier to transport." With that, he turned on his heel and headed out of the room with the shaggy one on his heels. The other pulled out a syringe and came straight for her. She struggled, but it wasn't much of a fight.

Within minutes, Jade again greeted oblivion.

Jamie Targaet

Jamie Targaet is the author of the Hounds of Hell MC. She's anxious to introduce you to this club of gorgeous, dominant men and the lucky women who surrender to them. The ride is going to get wild at times, not going to lie. But there's thrilling action, scorching hot sex scenes, and all the feels.

Jamie writes erotic romance for Changeling Press, a little fanfiction on the side, and she's an aspiring horror writer in another life. She enjoys time with her family (including the fur babies). She likes good horror movies and shows, emo metal and classic rock, and time spent in other worlds writing and reading. She loves hearing from readers and is looking forward to hearing from you.

Jamie Targaet at Changeling Press:
changelingpress.com/jamie-targaet-a-227

Axe (Devoted Guardians MC 1)
A Dixie Reapers Shifter MC Romance
Harley Wylde & Jessica Coulter Smith

Emma -- I'm a coward. I know it. Being with Josh is nothing but one long nightmare, and I need to leave him, but I can't escape. He'll hunt me down, and I'll pay. I've survived for the sake of our son, Cody, but how much longer can I hold out? I'm not afraid to admit I need help, but do I dare reach out to someone? Moving to a new town might give me the opportunity. I just need to find the courage to run.

Axe -- As an alpha wolf shifter, I've lived a long time. I have my brothers in the Devoted Guardians MC, and the townspeople of Wolf Creek. What I don't have is a mate and family of my own. So, I give back where I can. I accept an assignment to mentor a kid who needed a Big Wolf. Instead, I find the family I've always wanted. Emma is my mate. My wolf knows it. But she's in trouble. Before I can claim her, I need to get her away from the abusive human she's with. Then I'll tackle the biggest issue of all -- Emma has no idea shifters exist.

Prologue

Emma

I brushed the hair back from my son's face, wishing I had the courage to change things. I didn't know how I'd explain the bruises on my body tomorrow, and I knew my perceptive little man would ask. He knew about his father's temper. Anyone within hearing range would. It wasn't something I could hide very well.

Josh had been so nice when I'd first met him. He'd lured me in with false promises. When I'd told him about the baby, he'd thrown a fit, called me names, and stormed out of my life. I'd spent too many nights praying and begging for him to come back, thinking it would improve our lives. I should have known better. Bitterness welled inside me.

Money was the only reason he'd returned. I'd had a decent job, and while it was barely enough to scrape by, he'd thought I was his ticket to sitting around doing nothing all day. I'd proven him right until I'd lost my job. The pandemic that swept the nation a year ago had devastating results. Not only loss of loved ones, for those who had families, but also the closing of many small businesses.

Josh blamed me, even though I'd had nothing to do with any of it. Somehow, it was still my fault I didn't have a job anymore. It wasn't that I hadn't applied places -- because I had. For every opening, there were twenty or more applicants. Which was why I now found myself in a small town in the Georgia mountains, around two hours from Atlanta. The nearest town with a big chain store was a place called Ashton Grove. It wasn't a big town by any means, but far larger than Wolf Creek.

"I'm so sorry, baby," I murmured to my son. Little Cody was only seven, nearly eight, and he'd already been through so much.

I smelled the stench of alcohol and knew Josh was on the move again. I'd locked the door to Cody's room when I came inside, hoping to avoid the man I'd come to hate with every fiber of my being. If Wolf Creek had a women's shelter, or even a homeless shelter, I'd have taken Cody and left. As it was, we had nowhere to go and were stuck living in this hell with a man I wished would die.

"Emma! Get your ass out here!"

"Be quiet, Josh. You'll wake up Cody."

I bit my lip when I heard his fist hit the door several times, and his roar of outrage. Cody's eyes flew open, and I pressed my finger to his lips so he'd remain quiet. He gave me a nod, and I knew he understood what was going on. He'd witnessed his father's rage far too many times. Although Josh usually reserved the worst of his abuse for the times Cody wasn't around.

I wished there was a way for Cody to have a good male influence in his life, but since I didn't have any family or any friends around town, that wasn't likely to happen anytime soon. Although, I'd noticed a flyer at the library for a program called Big Wolf Little Wolf. I'd thought it a cute play on words with the town name and had memorized the number.

Tomorrow, I'd call and sign up Cody. If Josh found out, he'd be furious, so we'd have to be careful. It was the least I could do for my son. He needed to see what a real man was like and have someone worthy of being emulated. I'd rather die than have him turn out like his father.

I heard Josh's steps as he stumbled away and

knew he'd pass out soon. With some luck, he'd be gone in the morning because I had to take Cody to school. I closed my eyes and cuddled with my sweet boy.

If anyone is listening, I could really use some help. Please. Help us get away from him.

Chapter One

Axe

I stared at the message on my phone and scanned the area again. I'd agreed to meet my new Little Wolf at the park. The agency said the mom seemed nervous, and I could understand. Having a strange man meet with you and your kid had to be frightening. Even though the agency vetted everyone, I admired the woman for being cautious.

Just to be safe, I messaged the program director. She could send the mom a picture of me and let her know I was nearby. I'd had more than one mom freak out when I got close to their kid. Didn't matter I was an alpha wolf. Our special town didn't have one pack. It had many. Only certain wolves, like me and a few others, could handle being around other alphas without feeling the need to fight for dominance. Which was why not just any shifter would be permitted to move here. Each alpha had to pass a series of tests and interviews.

I finally spotted a kid who matched the picture the agency sent. Cody Carter. He looked small for his age. Most eight-year-old shifters were much bigger. Even if it looked like he wouldn't officially be eight for another week, he still shouldn't look so scrawny. Even rabbit shifters and deer weren't as fragile in appearance as this kid.

Approaching the swings, I stopped a few feet away. From the corner of my eye, I saw a pretty blonde pop up from a nearby bench, her tense posture alerting me to the fact this had to be her son. She hadn't so much as twitched until I approached the boy.

"You Cody?" I asked.

"Yes, sir."

I smiled, liking how polite he was. His mother must have raised him right. "My name is Alexander, but everyone calls me Axe. I'm with the Big Wolf Little Wolf program."

Cody's eyes went wide. "Really?"

I nodded. "Yep. I thought we could get to know each other a bit today, and maybe set up our next visit."

The swing stopped, and Cody shifted on the seat. He cast a furtive glance at his mother before focusing on me again. I wondered about that quick look but maintained eye contact with the kid. Until the breeze shifted. Every muscle in my body locked up tight, and my eyes shifted to that of my wolf. I felt a rumbling growl build inside me as the sweetest scent filled my nose. My mouth watered and my fangs ached. *What the fuck*? I'd never had such a reaction to a simple scent before.

The sound of dry grass crunching drew my attention to Cody's mom. And that's when I realized how truly fucked I was -- because the tantalizing smell was coming from Emma Carter. I breathed in deeper and realized something was seriously wrong. These two didn't have a drop of shifter blood in them. In fact, they were one hundred percent human. What the hell were they doing in Wolf Creek?

She tugged at her sleeves and crossed her arms, then dropped them to her sides again. The way she shifted from foot to foot told me her fight-or-flight response was kicking in. She might not realize I was a predator, but something inside her could feel it. Didn't matter, I wouldn't hurt her. I'd sooner cut off my paw.

The woman jolted and pulled her phone from her pocket. The way her face relaxed told me it was likely the text from the program director. Better later than never, but the timing sucked. I should have held back and not approached for another minute or two, given them time to reach out to her. Perhaps she wouldn't have been as frightened.

She turned her face away, and it felt like someone had punched me in the gut. Even though she'd done her best to hide it, I could see the bruising under her makeup. Some asshole had dared put their hands on her? I'd slaughter them!

The intensity of my feelings startled me, and I nearly took a step back. Sure, I hated the thought of anyone abusing a woman or kid, but not once had I reacted like this. Something seemed different about these two, and I wasn't entirely certain what it was. If this were a fairy tale, I'd say I'd just found my mate. Except fated mates didn't really exist. This town was proof enough. Shifters paired up much the same as humans did, with the caveat that it would be forever. We didn't believe in divorce, which meant we entered relationships with a shit ton of caution. And yet... every breath I took pulled in more of her scent, and the longer I looked at the bruising on her skin, the angrier I became. No, anger didn't encompass the emotion. Rage. Pure hatred for whoever had touched her.

My gums ached and saliva pooled in my mouth. My beast wanted to sink his teeth into the person responsible and rend him limb from limb. I decided it had to be a "he." Even our most volatile female wouldn't have done this, and a human woman wouldn't have done so much damage. Otherwise, I felt certain Emma would have been able to dodge the blow or run away.

I took a deep breath. Then another. Slowly, I calmed the wolf inside me before he decided to come all the way out. The last thing I needed to do was scare either of them. Something told me neither of these two knew about shifters. I forced myself to smile and wave at Emma.

"I'm Axe Tremaine. You must be Cody's mom, Emma. It's nice to meet the both of you. I was just telling Cody that I'm with Big Wolf Little Wolf."

Her eyes widened, and her lips parted. "You're the one they sent? I thought…"

Part of me wanted to be offended, but compared to her tiny stature, I probably seemed like a huge beast. Pretty accurate. Despite the wolf lurking under my skin, I still wouldn't have done something like beat on someone weaker than me. Whoever had hurt her needed to be taught a lesson. Or possibly buried in the woods after being torn apart. I was leaning toward option two at the moment.

"Guess I'm not what you imagined."

She pressed her fingers to her lips and paled a little. "I'm sorry. I'm being rude, and you came here to meet Cody. You're just… bigger than I anticipated. The picture they sent made you seem smaller."

My eyebrows went up, and she showed me the text from the program director. I snorted and tried damn hard not to laugh. Yeah, I didn't know what Shelly was up to. Why the hell had she sent a picture that was from before I became a full-fledged adult? It didn't make any sense. I knew she had a newer one. In fact, this program hadn't even existed back then. Of course, the fact she'd known me since I was a snot-nosed brat didn't help matters any.

"You'll have to pardon Shelly. She probably thought it was funny and didn't realize the difference might startle you," I said. For that matter, I doubted she knew they were human. "I'll have a word with her later."

I'd speak to her about several things. Starting with why the fuck she'd allowed someone to join the program without interviewing them in person. If she had, she'd have known immediately that neither of them was a shifter. Then I needed to have a chat with the mayor to discover how humans had been allowed into town in the first place.

"I thought for this first visit, we could get to know each other a little and maybe Cody could give me some ideas of what he'd like to try next time. We could go to a movie, a sporting event, come back to the park... It's entirely up to him." I smiled at the kid, and he grinned back. The more I looked at him, the more I realized he'd suffered too. Maybe not in the same way his mom had, but the kid was too thin and had dark smudges under his eyes from not sleeping well. Did that mean his father still lived with them? Was he the one hurting Emma?

Shit. Things were getting more complicated by the second.

"We're new to this," Emma said. "Well, new to town too."

I didn't know how to bring up Cody's father. Each situation was different. With shifters, they seldom used the Big Wolf Little Wolf service unless the father died. Otherwise, shifters were always a part of their kids' lives. Only a rare few were shitty parents. Although, there were times when a man was too busy providing for his family to do the fun things like attend class trips, teach them how to play ball or drive a car, and other things you'd expect a parent to handle. In those times, they'd use the program to make sure their little shifters received all the help they needed.

No one looked down on those who used the Big Wolf Little Wolf program. It was a service the community needed and one I was proud to be a part of. Same went for my brothers in the Devoted Guardians MC. Although, we weren't like the typical motorcycle clubs I'd seen in other places. Yes, we had a clubhouse, and we rode our motorcycles almost everywhere. But we weren't an outlaw club. Just a group of guys who held common beliefs. A brotherhood.

Emma eyed my cut, and I wondered if I should have left it behind and driven the truck here. Since I hadn't thought I'd be leaving the park with Cody, I'd brought my Harley Davidson Fat Bob. Knowing she was human and new to town, I'd have done things differently if someone had mentioned those two things earlier. Humans tended to see my cut and thought of the popular TV show *Sons of Anarchy*, and my club was so far from that.

"Yes, I'm in a motorcycle club. No, it's not like what you've watched or read. I promise, your kid is safe with me."

She gave a short nod and worried at her bottom lip. I could tell she wasn't sure if she should believe me. Couldn't blame her. Clearly, the asshole who'd bruised her face hadn't given her much confidence in men.

"Can we get ice cream?" Cody asked, his eyes wide and pleading.

"I'm good with that." I put my hands in my pockets. "As long as your mom says it's okay. The ice cream shop is just down the street. The three of us could walk there."

"Cody, we talked about this before," Emma said softly.

The crestfallen expression on his face tugged at my heart. "Is he not allowed to have any?"

She shook her head. "It's not that. Like I said, we just moved here, and Cody's dad just started a job."

Ah, so it was a money thing. "It's my treat. Both of you can get whatever you want."

I could see she wanted to agree. It only took her another minute before she nodded, and Cody smiled from ear to ear.

The little boy jumped off the swing and ran over to me, grabbing hold of my hand. I closed my fingers around his much smaller ones, and instinctively reached for Emma's. I heard her soft gasp but noticed she didn't pull away. Together, the three of us went to Martha's, the best -- and only -- ice cream parlor in town. And it felt more right than anything ever had in my entire life.

I was so fucked.

Bad Boys Multiverse
A Bad Boy Romance
Dixie Reapers MC
Devil's Boneyard MC
Hades Abyss MC
Devil's Fury MC
Bryson Corners
Owned by the Mob
Reckless Kings MC
Devoted Guardians MC
Savage Raptors MC
Devil's Boneyard MC Audio
Dixie Reapers MC Print
Dixie Reapers MC Audio
Hades Abyss MC Audio

Jessica Coulter Smith

Award-winning author Jessica Coulter Smith has been in love with the written word since she was a child writing her first stories in crayon. Today she's a multi-published author of over seventy-five novellas and novels. Romance is an integral part of her world, and she firmly believes that love will find you at the right time, even if Mr. Right is literally out of this world.

Jessica Coulter Smith at Changeling Press:
changelingpress.com/jessica-coulter-smith-a-144

Grimdarke (Maw of Mayhem MC 1)
A Maw of Mayhem MC Shifter Romance
AK Nevermore

Out of options and on the run after her psychotic father's released from prison, Kit Parson heads to the only place she might be safe from him, the Maw of Mayhem MC. The unexpected move buys her time, but also puts her at risk. Surrounded by shifters, her inner cat begs to be released, and after witnessing a brutal attack on her mother as a child, she refuses to let the monster out. Totally doable, provided no bodily fluids are ever exchanged.

That takes the MC's hot-as-hell VP, Grimdarke James, officially off the table. Mourning the recent murder of the club's alpha and struggling to control his inner cat, the tattooed Viking god is on thin ice. If he goes feral again, he'll be put down. Which makes his cat's insistence that Kit belongs to him problematic, upsetting the delicate balance of the MC's internal politics, and the woman blackmailing Grim.

But when Kit's father catches up with her, Grim has no choice but to trust his cat, and Kit can't deny their chemistry. Can they hold on to each other when everything is trying to tear them apart? After a gruesome triple murder propels them deeper into the paranormal world, they find themselves with unlikely allies, even as their enemies threaten to destroy everything they hold dear.

Before

Bass thumped, heavy and hot, throbbing up through the soles of Grim's shit kickers. The club's black lights flickered with the beat, highlighting the sweat-slicked bodies undulating in a writhing mass of lust and abandon below him.

He leaned back against the balcony's bar, vibing enough "don't fuck with me" to keep all but the brain-dead sluts off him. Not that he could blame them, but he didn't tend to stick his dick in stupid. Or anything else.

-- laughing --

Happy about that, you furry motherfucker?

Fucking cat was out of control. Grim scanned the pit of simmering sex below, the stink of human desire thick in his nose. He turned to his alpha, not fucking impressed, or in the mood for bullshit. "This is what we rode five hours for?"

Clay gave a slow nod, more close-lipped than usual, totally fixated on one of the Lucite pillars rising from the dance floor. Grim shook his head and took another sip of his overpriced beer. Clay'd spill when he was ready and not a moment before. There had to be a damned good reason for them to be there, and if he wanted to stare at an empty platform, more power to him. The others had plenty of eye candy to enjoy.

And human or not, those dancers could move, their getups not leaving much to the imagination. Fishnets, booty shorts, and shredded Ts reading "Skin" straining across their tits as they worked the poles in the center of each platform.

But as much as he approved on principle, his dick couldn't care less.

[*SMUG*]

Fuck his cat and this shit. He downed the last of his beer and cracked the glass onto the bar. "Gotta piss."

Grim shouldered past, and Clay grunted, still fixated on that platform. Whatever had caught the alpha's attention had brought his cat close to the surface. He wasn't going anywhere.

Grim pushed through the crowd, shrugging off roaming hands and bodies pressing close. Whispered promises and innuendo fell on deaf ears. One brazen stolen kiss, and a tongue laced with the tang of a narcotic tangled with his. He spun the woman back into the throng and spat.

Hall for the john was packed, moans coming from the men's room. He shouldered past the line for the ladies', through the door.

"Hey! You can't --"

Yeah, he could. A dozen stalls, all closed. Wide eyes watching him in the mirror, lipstick and mascara dropping, their owners scurrying back like vermin, gasping as he unzipped and started pissing into the sink. Grim's head tipped back with a long exhale. Fuuuck --

A flush and slam of a stall door opening. The water in the sink beside him crashed on. He glanced over. A petite, raven-haired woman dressed like the podium dancers beneath a man's oversized, unzipped hoodie soaped up her hands. Grim pursed his lips at her sinful curves. God freaking damn…

"You know that's not a urinal, right?" she asked, her reflection glaring at him in the mirror. Or more accurately, glaring at his cut.

Her whiskey-dark eyes flicked up and met his. Grim's mouth went dry. His dick twitched as he shoved it back into his jeans. She didn't drop her gaze.

"Desperate times." Grim's voice rumbled, his inner beast sitting up and taking notice, along with his cock. *Are you fucking kidding me?*

-- want --

Now *you want*? He barked out a laugh. The shit on that chick's tongue must've been a premium grade miracle.

Little miss five-foot-nothing-and-not-into-bikers reached past him to slap on the water in his sink, rinsing it down. "That's fucking disgusting. You need to leave before I call security."

Damn, she was a live one. Grim crowded into her space, and she didn't budge, glaring up at him with her hands on her hips, just begging for him to smack that ass. He wet his lips and stroked down the side of her cheek, trailing to her quickening pulse. Her hand snaked up to grab his wrist, and a jolt went through him, cock kicking against his zipper.

The ebony of her pupils blew out, eating away the warmth of her irises. The scent of her arousal flooded his nose. Her breath caught, then stuttered out, a little crease appearing between her brows. "D-don't touch me."

"Stop wanting me to," he murmured, tilting up her mouth to his.

Her fist took him in the jaw, and he stumbled back. The fuck?

-- YESSS --

Within, his beast coiled to pounce as she flung open the bathroom door, storming out --

Gunshots.

Clay.

Grim's cat scrabbled to get out. The beast's consciousness slammed into his, overwhelming him with the desire to shift and charge through the crowd, rending and tearing until he --

The hallway erupted with people frantic to escape, and the woman fell back into the bathroom. He lunged forward to steady her, the press of her body against his distracting the beast long enough for him to wrestle back control. She wriggled away, and Grim slammed the door shut and locked it, panting. Shit, that was close...

[ANGER]

We're not shifting here. He needed to think, not react, Goddamn it. He pulled his cell, then shoved it back into his pocket. Fuck. They'd ridden down alone. MC wouldn't be able to back them up for hours. He raked a hand through his shaggy blond hair and pulled his piece, listening for a break in the deluge of bodies streaming past the door.

Movement to his right. The woman had flattened herself against the far wall. Grim rocked his jaw. She had one hell of a hook, and a set of legs to match. Damned if they weren't tight as fuck...

"Don't even think about it, asshole," she gritted out, eyeing his gun.

Grim smirked, shifting his cock. Oh, he was thinking about it, all right. Her peaked nipples and the way she rubbed her thighs together said he wasn't the only one.

-- Clay --

Right. Wasn't the fucking time. Head in the game. The rush outside the door had dissipated, and Grim raised his gun, fingers on the doorknob. He glanced back at her.

"Stay here."

She rolled her eyes, arms crossed over what had to be all natural DDs.

Goddamn.

-- want --

Later. He unlocked the door and eased it open, then slid --

She burst out from behind him and was gone before the door slammed against the wall. A smile tipped up his lips, his proverbial tail twitching. Any other situation, he'd chase that down and tag it. Fucking figured he and his cat would agree on something now.

The hall was deserted, a lone cocktail napkin fluttering abandoned in the pulsing lights. Grim's jaw clenched, the shit music drowning out any sounds from the balcony above. His finger inched toward the trigger, the dusky scent of cat edging out the reek of humanity in the room.

Mother. Fucker.

He crept up the stairs to the balcony --

"I done told you what would happen, Claymore, laying rights on what ain't yours to claim. Destiny always takes its due."

Grim's foot paused on the last step, his stomach dropping at the gravelly deep woods drawl. No -- Asshole had close to four more years in the pen --

"Fuck you." Clay gritted out, his voice racked with pain.

"Mmm, think I'll fuck that ol' lady of yours instead. Heard Marie ain't much for conversatin' these days, but I ain't never been real interested in what she had t'say."

Grim ducked into an alcove behind the curtain of the VIP section. Swearing and a scuffle sounded over the pounding techno beat, then the sharp crack of flesh on flesh.

Man laughed at Clay's agonized groan. "Easy... knock that blade free, an' you'll ruin the scene. Let's stretch this out a tick. Shiv, kill that Godawful shit."

A semi-automatic fired and the music cut out, the silence a deafening void.

Grim nosed the dusky velvet curtain aside with the barrel of his gun, peeking through. Cold sweat drenched his body, cat trying to tuck tail. He fought to kill the whine scrabbling to burst from his insides. Wishing like hell his eyes hadn't confirmed what his churning guts already knew.

Reaper was out.

[FEAR]

Yeah. They were fucked. Totally fucking fucked.

Across the room, a half dozen brothers from their rival MC, Satan's Vengeance, were raiding the bar with one eye on the show. Grapple, Reaper's enforcer, had Clay on his knees, one massive hand ripping the alpha's head back to bare his throat.

The other was on a silver knife buried to the hilt in Clay's shoulder.

That son of a bitch.

Grim swallowed bile, shoving away the memory of that burn. Black fire webbing decay through his flesh, paralyzing his beast --

-- run --

No. Let me think. Shit was easier said than done, but -- how'd they know to hit them at the club tonight?

Unless the MC had a rat... or a Mouse. Fucking tech nerd was supposed to be keeping tabs on the prison. Anger stilled the tremor in his hand, and Grim blinked the sweat from his eyes. Because if Reaper and his brothers were here, they hadn't just been betrayed by one of their own, they'd been offered up on a silver fucking platter as sacrifices.

How the hell had the psycho prick gotten out?

The lanky biker sniffed, running a hand under

his nose. Grim tensed at the smirk tipping up the asshole's lips, keenly aware of the stink of his own fear. Reaper snagged a bottle from one of his boys. His rings clanked against the glass as he imbibed, that icy blue gaze, dead as skittering leaves, sweeping the shadows -

- until it met Grim's.

Reaper's lips twitched again. "Ah. Now that we're all here --"

He raised his gun and blew away half of Clay's skull.

Chapter One

Upstate New York in the fall was beautiful, and it made Kit want to puke.

She gripped the steering wheel tighter, her sweaty palms slicking the leather, and glanced in her rearview, then at her phone's GPS. No service -- again. Damn it. This was not where she wanted to be...

Wait. Signs for a trailhead were coming up. *Thank you, sweet baby Jesus.* She pulled onto the shoulder, staring blankly at the plexi-covered map tacked onto the tiny shelter in front of the car. Woodbine Swamp Trail. Shit. She'd missed the turn-off for the house. Ugh! How could everything in this shit town look the same and so frickin' different all at once?!

Fifteen years will do that, genius.

Her forehead dropped to the steering wheel, bumping it thrice. Stupid. Stupid. Stupid. She couldn't do this. She couldn't --

Goddamnit, girl, grow a pair!

Enough. Wasn't like she had a choice. She pushed back in her seat and slapped the car in reverse, hoping like hell there wasn't anything behind her. Frickin' hatchback was stuffed to the gills with the sad remains of her life, and she wasn't up for losing any more of it.

Kit dashed away a tear. And whose fault was that?

She just had to blow shit up. Couldn't duck her head and keep punching numbers, because *lay low* was too big of a fucking ask. Nope, fuck overtime at the accounting firm, had to go out there and twerk her ass at the club, knowing full well that milkshake wasn't gonna bring anything but trouble to her yard.

Her mind leapt to that tall drink of golden Viking god pissing in a sink, covered in tattoos and oozing temptation. Yup. Case in point, and as much as it shocked the shit out of her, she'd been into him.

So fucking into him, like, wanted him into her.

Not happening.

She bit at a cuticle, trying to ignore the very real possibility she was about to deliver herself to his doorstep, and the fact that her panties had just soaked clean through.

Son of a -- Chanté would quip something about chickens coming home to roost, but they weren't even Kit's damned chickens. And why the fuck chickens? Woman was NYC born and raised, you'd think she'd have useless witticisms about pigeons.

Damn, though. He was fiiine...

Stop it.

You'd think she'd be more concerned about the shifter shadowing her for the past two weeks... the one whose face starred in her nightmares. Reaper hadn't approached her, but his message was clear, and like a fucking cat, he'd been playing with her.

... Run, little mouse...

Kit's teeth clenched at the memory of her father's gravelly twang. She put the car in gear and kept driving in the wrong direction. Away from the house, toward the last damned place she wanted to go, and the only place she had left. Two weeks of couch surfing and shitty motels had made that abundantly clear, and her flat fucking broke.

Back to the scene of the crime, the one place she hoped like hell he didn't have the balls to go back to.

Motorcycles rumbled in the distance and her gut threatened to rebel, cold sweat pebbling her skin. She licked the anxiety from her lips.

The rumble grew, and a moment later a stream of leather and exhaust whipped by her as a convoy of bikes sped past, heading back toward civilization. A manic giggle burbled from her throat, and she took a slow --

Shit! Gas pedal, girl, you gotta keep your shit together...

Focus. Drive to the damned compound. One more mile.

... And keep it together. Hah! Fat fucking chance. She blew out a breath, her temples thudding with the beginnings of a migraine. Goddamn. After all those years of praying to be out from under Claymore James's thumb... this had not been part of the fantasy.

Getting shit-faced, twerking on his grave, and then setting the MC's compound on fire, yes. Pulling up to the chain-link gate and asking to see Mud Knuckle?

Nope. Can't say that'd made the list, but here she was.

I mean really, Mud Knuckle? Kit sighed, rubbing a temple. If she needed any further confirmation her life had officially gone to shit: Ta-frickin'-da.

One of the dopey-looking prospects manning the gate eyed her, pursing his lips. The scraggly little pornstache he was rocking made his mouth look like a porcupine's asshole.

Moron leaned in her window. "Ain't no muddy knuckles here." He snickered, shooting his zit-infested buddy a look.

Kit sighed. Great, they were gonna fuck with her.

"Nah," Zits said, ambling closer to leer. "But I ain't opposed to rectifyin' that situation." He grinned, making a lewd gesture.

Whoo. Ten points for originality there, son. She

rolled her eyes and unbuckled her seatbelt. It was showtime. The two high school rejects scrambled back, wide-eyed when she threw open the door and got out, leaving the hoodie she'd permanently borrowed from Chanté on the seat. Fuck, it was hypothermia cold.

"What? I thought we was 'wreck-t-fyin' that sits-e-ate-shon,'" she finger quoted, mimicking his dipshit twang and cocking a hip.

Pornstache's throat bobbed, taking in her tight tee and yoga pants. God, men were pigs. Pathetic, predictable pigs. Flash them braless DDs, and their brains shorted out faster than a hairdryer in a bathtub. Add the fact that her nipples were hard enough to cut glass, and the poor boys didn't stand a chance.

"Uh, yeah." Pornstache tugged on his cut and cleared the squeak from his throat. Slack-jawed, Zits smacked his shoulder, earning himself a glare. "I mean, hell yeah. We're down, baby."

Kit arched her back, stretching. Damn, that felt good after five hours behind the wheel. Pornstache groaned like he was about to wreck-t-fy in his pants. She sauntered over and ran a finger down his sternum.

"Then how 'bout you boys open the gate so I can move my car out of the way and get down to business."

Zits moved so fast he just about face-planted rushing to unlatch the big chain-link section on wheels blocking the compound's access road. He'd pulled it halfway across the pavement by the time Kit got back into her car. Pornstache shook his head like a dog, blinking as the door clunked shut, and he stumbled over to help his buddy.

Suckers.

Kit almost felt bad as she drove past, waggling her fingers.

Okay, no, she didn't. She wriggled back into the hoodie, one hand on the wheel and shivering. Her stomach churned as she drove around the last bend to the chapter house, half expecting the entire club to be out there waiting for her. The woods opened up --

And the lot was empty.

Of frickin' course it was empty. The funeral was today. Now. She could still make it. Wasn't that why she'd blown out of the city so fast? To spit on Claymore's grave like she'd told Chanté she was going to? Get some kind of fucked-up closure?

Yeah, has nothing to do with the fact you're being stalked by a psycho.

Kit bit back a sob, coasting the last few hundred feet to a stop in front of the long, two-storied building. It was ugly. A dark, cinderblock gray, squatting against a barren hillside. She bit her lip, eyes flicking to the last window on the left, waiting for the shitty mini blinds to part.

They didn't. Wouldn't.

Dead. Everything looked fucking dead. Probably because it was.

Fuck this shit. She jerked up the emergency brake and killed the engine. Slammed the door open, then shut. Stomped across the half-frozen muddy lot, odd bits of gravel and glass crunching beneath her boots. Eyes fixed on the burnt-out jaws scored into the surface of the MC's chapter house door, she approached the belly of the beast -- and stepped into the Maw of Mayhem.

* * *

Grim stood beside an open grave, looking anywhere but at the casket.

Low fieldstone walls. Tumbled tombstones green with lichen and pitted with age, the epitaphs worn smooth. Craggy, unkempt trees jagged their roots out like lightning between monoliths and statuary, skewing the cobblestone path akimbo. And in the far corner, a small chapel with arched, diamond-paned windows. It hunched half-hidden in a copse of trees, its brick-red cathedral-style door slightly ajar, taunting him with what was inside.

Nah, check that. More like threatening him with a who.

[*ANGER*]

Fuck her.

Sights seen, he raised his flask, wrists still scabbed and swollen, ribs aching, numb to the burn as he swallowed. Goddamn, it was a shit day to bury someone.

-- whimpering --

Cold. Wet. Standing in mud up to his asshole. The smell of dead leaves, pending snow, and wood-burning stoves scraping down the back of his throat. Stinging his eyes -- he shot a hand across his face and pinched the bridge of his nose.

Fuck. Keep telling yourself that's why you're tearing up, you pussy. Sure as hell wasn't the shit sermon he'd just sat through, and the priest's sanctimonious second act graveside wasn't any better. Fucking civ.

His sonorous drone alone deserved a beatdown. Prick wasn't even attempting to veil his contempt. You'd think a man of God would have more tact, or at least more sense. The graveyard was a sea of leathers. There had to be close to two hundred patches crammed in graveside. The white-on-black fanged Maw of Mayhem was predominant, but plenty of cuts from associate MCs were in attendance, and the atmosphere was dense with grief and some seriously dank bud.

Shit, maybe that would chill his cat the fuck out. Whiskey sure as hell wasn't, and his inner beast was moodier than a teenaged girl.

"... through our Lord Jesus Christ, we commend to Almighty God our brother Nathaniel *Claymore* James..." The priest's tongue curdled around the name. Motherfucker was just asking to get hit --

-- *YESSS* --

Grim's hackles rose, fur bristling from his nape. Goddamn it. *No.*

Not fucking here, and not fucking now. He shoved the beast back down, spinning from the grave and stalking to the edge of the crowd. Brothers gave him a wide berth and curt nods as he passed, their ol' ladies laying on the sympathetic moues, inevitability in their eyes.

Just waiting for him to lose it.

Grim gritted his teeth, trembling hand scraping back the hair from his eyes. He wasn't gonna lose it, and he didn't want their fucking pity.

What he wanted was for his alpha -- damn it, his fucking father -- not to be rotting in a Goddamned box. Short of that, he'd take doling out the same fate to the asshole that put Clay in there, and this fucking circus wasn't getting him any closer to that goal.

Not that he'd been able to pull the trigger when he'd had a chance.

The memory of Reaper's alpha command paralyzing him while his brothers beat the shit out of him spiked rage-fueled fear up Grim's spine, making him hyperaware of every lingering contusion.

Why the fuck hadn't they ended him?

From the side-eye he was getting, he wasn't the only one that wanted to know.

"... though we are sinners, you wish always to

hear us. Accept the prayers we offer in sadness for your servant Nathaniel *Claymore*..."

[*ANGER*]

A growl rumbled through Grim's chest. That was it. Priest was about to be introduced to his own hole in the ground --

A hand clamped down on his shoulder. Stitch. The club's sergeant-at-arms' rheumy oyster gaze bored into him, his voice a low rumble. "That priest ain't worth losing it over, and we got a situation."

Grim shrugged out of his grip. "No shit, and I'm fine."

"Bull." Man snorted, heating up his vape. "And I ain't talkin' about this clusterfuck. Them two chuckleheads we left manning the gate let some chick in."

"They stupid?" Grim dragged a hand down his face. Dumb question.

"She asked to see MK."

"What the fuck does she want to see Mud Knuckle for?"

Stitch took a hit, lips thinning as he held it, and shrugged. "Dunno." He exhaled. "But hear tell she was hot as hades, mid-twenties, and her car was crammed full of shit. Maybe another one of his by-blows comin' home to roost?"

Great. Grim pounded the last of what was in his flask. Because the first one that'd showed up was such a fucking prize.

Stitch chuckled for all the wrong reasons. "Nikki's a snake, but tell me you ain't thinking about a sister sandwich. Fuck, if this one's as hot as her --"

"I'm not. After all the shit she's pulled --"

"Whatever, kid. We both know that for better or for worse, that pussy's got you whipped. You know

my money's on worse, but that ain't here nor there."
He frowned, rubbing his forehead. "Peel off. Go get
your dick sucked. She's around, ain't she?"

Grim glanced at the chapel. Yeah, she was here
all right, wanting to cash in on their deal. He just
wanted it to end. Stitch was spot-on about her being a
snake. She'd slithered back into the club's good graces
with some bullshit Come-to-Jesus act while Grim'd
been laid up the hospital, claiming they'd made
amends and acting like his queen. Jesus fuck, his
father's body wasn't even in the ground. Dealing with
her shit was the last thing he wanted to do.

"Fuck her," he muttered.

Stitch's eyebrow rose as he cleared his carb. "I
ain't gonna hold my breath on that count. Else you
woulda come clean to the club about your deal with
her already. Ask me, it's high time you do. Clay's in
that box yonder. Ain't nothing you confess is gonna
hurt him."

Grim kicked at a chunk of frozen mud. Maybe
not, but Stitch didn't know all the details. Nikki did,
and her spilling had the potential of planting Grim
right beside Clay.

"You know," Stitch mused, "She's sportin' a bite.
Says it's yours. One way or another, you need to
address the shit she's pullin', quick."

Fucking manipulative -- Bite wasn't his, not that
he could publicly dispute it. Grim jammed his hands
wrist deep into his pockets, wishing he could smack
her shit down, but the bitch had him by the balls and
liked to yank.

Stitch sighed out his hit. "Christ, at least go for a
run. You gotta let that beast of yours out."

No shit, and the thought of pounding through
the mountains on four paws --

[*JOY*]

-- but fuck, add it to the Goddamned list of shit he had to deal with since Clay'd been executed. Grim scratched his bristled jaw.

"Priority's not on my dick or a run, it's making Satan's Vengeance pay."

The old man took another hit and inspected the tip of his vape. "Gonna be pretty hard to take out an entire MC if you're all by your lonesome. Nikki's shit aside, way it went down with Clay... brothers want answers I know you ain't keen to give."

Grim looked away. "I told 'em what happened."

"Yeah, but not the why."

"Why the fuck does Reaper do anything?" he snarled, getting in Stitch's face. "He left me breathing to fuck with people's heads." Including Grim's. That Goddamned alpha command forcing his obedience... How the hell was he gonna lead the MC if another alpha could bend him over with a word?

Which meant Reaper wasn't done with him -- not by a long shot.

Stitch didn't bat an eye. "You're alive 'cause you're his kin. Man's a sadist, no argument there, but nepoticide ain't in him."

"Don't be so sure about that," Grim muttered, wincing at the lancing pain through his ribs and hating himself for it. "And he's not my uncle."

Stitch snorted. "Maybe not by blood, but he loved Abigail somethin' fierce. Was a damned tragedy the way him and Clay fell out over your mama. Her dying broke the both of them... Fucking broke us all." He took another hit off his vape and glanced at Grim askance. "Some more than others."

Grim tensed and Stitch doubled down. "It's past time you came to an understandin' with that bitch-ass beast of yours and set all this shit rollin' down the hill to rights. You're as alpha as Clay was. Time to own it and kick that bitch Nikki to the curb."

How high was the old man? Grim and his cat understood each other just fine. He did his thing, and the furry fucker dealt with it… most of the time. He shook his head, not wanting to get it.

Stitch didn't seem to notice, or more like didn't care. "And that means coming clean, about *all* of it."

-- the concrete room was ice-cold, dark brown ridges of offal frozen to the gritty floor. His tongue scrapes at it, torn and weeping, broken claws scrabbling for something, anything, to fill the gnawing void in his belly. The steel door clangs open, and a molly saunters into the room yowling, tail high and pitched to the side --

Fur bristled at Grim's nape, and Stitch grabbed him by the scruff, staring him down. "And you need to do it soon. The shit that hit the fan when Clay manned up and claimed you as his son ain't gonna be dick in comparison, and if they figure out how close you are to goin' feral again… They'll hunt you the fuck down, and he ain't here to save your ass."

[*GRIEF*]

The beast retreated, and Grim growled, shrugging loose. No way was he ready to throw his PTSD on the table for everyone to paw through. Wasn't happening… unless Nikki spilled it. Grim swallowed his fear, needing more time. As long as she thought she was gonna be his queen, she'd stay mum.

And if she didn't?

Grim toed a gravestone.

"… May his soul and the souls of all the faithful departed, through the mercy of God, rest in peace. Amen."

Thank fuck.

The rumbled response of the crowd signaled the end of the service, and brothers started vying for Grim's eye, either to offer their condolences or assess his mental state. The first he didn't want, and the second would be fine, right after he personally put a bullet in each and every member of Satan's Vengeance, starting with Reaper.

And on that note…

"I gotta get outta here," he said to Stitch, eyeing the chapel door. "Gonna run back to the clubhouse --"

[JOY]

"-- grab the Indian and check out how deep MK's dick has got us in it this time."

Stitch grunted, slapping Grim's shoulder. "Clay'd like you takin' her out, but don't get lost. Ride starts in an hour. Club's gonna expect you to show and say some words about the man."

"Right." Grim turned away, gut clenching like he was gonna puke.

He kept his eyes glued to his boots on the way out of the cemetery. Say some words. What the fuck did they expect him to say? His father was dead. Shot in the face by a psycho prick that had Grim by the short hairs and the rest of the MC by extension.

Fuck.

He smacked the side of the cage Clay had taken his final ride in and shucked off his cut, thumbs running over its patch. *Boo-fucking-hoo, asshole. Suck it the fuck up.* Grim sighed. He should be grateful.

He should be dead.

Clay'd saved him, given him that first chance when he pulled him out of Reaper's basement, and then another after Grim's cat had fucked that up by going feral. He owed it to the man not to waste this one, needed to honor his memory, keep his shit together, and do this, 'cause Stitch was right -- he was on thin fucking ice.

Grim sniffled, pinching the bridge of his nose. Goddamn smoke. He tore off the rest of his shit and tossed it into the hearse. One of the brothers would make sure it got back to him. His body ached -- a mottled collection of color courtesy of his fucking "uncle" and the two shitheads he'd shared a womb with. The memorial ride was gonna be literal hell on wheels for his ribs.

Good. He fucking deserved it. He dropped to hands and knees, hissing back pain as joints popped and muscles shifted from his human form into that of a mountain lion. Colors bled from the landscape and the distance softened to a blur. Sounds multiplied and sharpened.

[*JOY JOY JOY*]

A fragrance teased his nose.

He sneezed. Shook his head. What the hell was that? His lips curled up over sharp canines, drawing the scent into his mouth. Something about it...

-- *want* --

He padded deeper into the forest on silent paws and broke into a run.

AK Nevermore

AK Nevermore enjoys operating heavy machinery, freebases coffee, and gives up sarcasm for Lent every year.

A Jane-of-all-trades, she's a certified chef, restores antiques, and dabbles in beekeeping when she's not reading voraciously or running down the dream in her beat-up camo Chucks.

Unable to ignore the voices in her head, and unwilling to become medicated, she writes Science Fiction and Fantasy full time.

AK pays the bills writing a copious amount of copy, along with a column on SFF. She belongs to the Authors Guild, is an RWA chapter board member, volunteers for far too many committees, teaches creative writing, and on the rare occasion, sleeps.

AK Nevermore at Changeling Press:
changelingpress.com/ak-nevermore-a-234

Ghost (Shiva's Road MC 1)
A Shiva's Road MC Romance
Dana Cask

Ghost -- Against my better judgment, I went to Chicago to meet my father. Instead I find a sexy siren who's fighting a daily struggle to survive. I claim her for my own the first chance I get, but that's when our troubles really start. She won't leave without my sister Rachel, her best friend, and I'm a long way from home and my brothers. When the bad guys attack, I'll do whatever it takes to keep them both.

Simone -- I need a way out. When Ghost arrives, I take a chance and ask him for help. But he's the son of the man who sells my body. I don't know how far I can trust him. My life and Rachel's hang in the balance. Ghost says he wants me by his side forever. I'm trusting him with our lives, but can I trust him with my heart?

Chapter One

Ghost

"This place is something else," Beowulf said over the sound of their idling bikes.

Ghost didn't respond, knowing his best friend didn't expect him to. He just stared at the place his mother had called home for the last twenty-five years. The McMansion and surrounding grounds presented a vulgar display of wealth against the suburban Chicago backdrop. The pink granite drive wound around the two-story house, lit by spotlights in the center of the immaculately manicured lawn. In bright sunlight, he'd no doubt need darker shades to withstand the glare of the mica-flecked walls and white shutters. He'd known about the setup from the intel Bytes had gathered on his father before they left the compound in Central Ohio, but seeing it in person shocked the man who had grown up dirt poor in a single-wide trailer on the Mescalero Apache Tribe Reservation.

"Name," snapped a male voice from a box built into the brick column to the left of the wrought black iron gate.

"Lucas Blackfoot," Ghost replied. His voice sounded rusty, even to his own ears.

"You were told to come alone."

Ghost shrugged, sure the security cameras would pick up his response.

After a long pause, the voice instructed, "Park your motorcycles in the open garage bay. You will be met at the interior door. Do not enter without one of my men to escort you, or you will be shot."

"Friendly type, your Pops." Wulf chuckled.

Ghost let his unease out by revving his old Harley. The Knucklehead vibrated the ground as the gate with a stylized W in the center pulled back to allow them entrance. They followed the drive to the right of the house, moving at a slow pace on the loose gravel, and found the place they were to leave their bikes without issue.

Almost as soon as they swung their legs over the fenders, a door at the far end of the garage opened. A limo occupied one bay. Midlife crisis cars sat in the remaining two, each of which probably cost more than Ghost had seen during his entire childhood.

A large bald man in a black suit he couldn't button over his flabby stomach -- a security drudge so stereotypical as to be laughable -- motioned them to come closer.

"What do you wanna bet he gets handsy?" Wulf said loud enough to be overheard.

Ghost grunted. This was gonna suck. He had planned to get in and out as quickly as possible, having minimal interaction with his sperm donor.

"Which one of you is Blackfoot?" the guard asked as they approached.

Like that wasn't obvious. Even a toddler could tell the black-haired Native American from the Nordic blond. "I am," Ghost replied.

"Your... companion... can wait here." The guard put a wealth of innuendo into the word *companion*, still trying to get a rise out of him.

"No." Ghost didn't make a threatening move, but he wasn't going into this house alone. He'd never spoken to Donald P. Willard, never went looking for his parents after his mother left the Reservation when he was eight. His father should be happy he'd only brought his best friend for backup. No way in hell would he allow himself to be separated from Wulf this early in the game.

"You come alone, or you don't come at all."

"Fine," said Wulf, "We'll be home in our beds by morning then."

The dumbass reached out to grab Ghost by the arm. "I said --"

Ghost grabbed the guard's hand by the thumb and bent it back. When the man tried to twist out of his grip, Ghost held on long enough to make sure the man knew Ghost was choosing to release him.

Another man, this one a little older and in better shape than the first, appeared in the doorway. "Problem?"

"He doesn't want to come quietly, boss," Dumbass said.

"Let him bring his little friend if it makes him feel better," the new arrival replied. "I'm sure they won't cause any trouble. Right, boys?"

"We're housebroken," Wulf assured him. "Can't say the same for your team though. Need a lesson in manners."

"Boss" stared at them for a few beats, then turned on his heel and walked back into the house. His lapdog followed, leaving Ghost and Wulf to take up the rear. As soon as they cleared the doorway, another man came up behind them, closing the door and walking practically on their heels. They moved through the mostly dark house in that formation until they reached a closed door with soft light spilling through around the cracks.

A knock on the door received a curt, "Enter."

A hand on his back pushed Ghost ahead of Wulf into the room. No less opulent than the rest of the house, the study had dark built-in shelves at the back wall and thick, velvet green drapes bracketing the floor-to-ceiling windows along the side. Donald P.

Willard sat behind a polished walnut desk. A Tiffany desk lamp illuminated Donald's thick features and extremely short-cropped, graying hair. His hands were laced together in front of him, resting over a sizeable belly straining the buttons on his tailored shirt. His blue suit jacket hung on the back of his leather executive chair. The picture of a prominent light-skinned black businessman, surrounding himself with obvious signs of wealth and opulence. Ghost was pretty sure it was all a front, meant to impress.

"Son, please have a seat. The rest of you are dismissed," Donald said.

The three bodyguards tried to grab Wulf to remove him bodily from the room, but he evaded their grasps and sat down on the green leather sofa which rested against a creamy damask wallpaper. "I think I'll stay. I like it here," Wulf said mildly.

"This is a private conversation between my son and myself. Please do us the courtesy of letting us have this family moment," Donald replied.

Wulf looked to Ghost, who gave him a slight nod. Beowulf could take care of himself, and it didn't seem like anyone was going to talk in front of his friend.

"Come on, boys. Show me the kitchen. I could use a snack after the long ride." Wulf jumped up from the couch and led the way out into the hall.

Once they were alone and the door shut, Donald gave Ghost an appraising glance. "You look like your mother."

Ghost knew what he meant. His father's African American heritage didn't show much in Ghost's features. There didn't seem much point in replying so Ghost didn't bother.

Donald sighed. "Have a seat, son. We have a lot

to talk about."

Ghost sat in one of the chairs in front of Donald's desk that matched the leather sofa. It was as uncomfortable as it looked. Still, he said nothing. He'd learned a long time ago prolonged silence had a way of getting people to start rambling just to fill the void.

"I have to say, your existence came as quite a shock to me. In all the years I've been married to Caroline, she never once mentioned you. Do you know why?"

"No."

"Has she ever contacted you since she left the Reservation?"

"No."

"I've always wanted a son to carry on my legacy. Surely, she would have known I'd have welcomed you with open arms."

Ghost shrugged. His mother had signed over custody of him to his grandfather when she left, giving no explanation. His memories of her were happy, but dim. He couldn't say why his mother did what she did, and wouldn't tell this man even if he did know. He owed this man nothing.

"Did she tell you anything about me before she left? Anything at all?"

"No." Ghost knew he sounded like a broken record but really what was there to say? He'd received word of his mother's death from a lawyer, closely followed by a summons from Donald P. Willard to discuss her "affairs." Ghost already regretted his decision to come here and couldn't wait to get the fuck out.

"Man of few words, eh? I can respect that. Too many people don't stand by their word these days. I'm not one of those. Old school to the core, just like my daddy." He probably practiced his "trust me" smile in the mirror. Ghost wasn't falling for it.

"Why am I here?" He knew why, but he wanted to see how the other man would spin it.

"I wanted to meet you, talk to you. I am your father, after all."

"Are you sure?" Ghost was. Bytes had done the research. Donald's name wasn't listed on his birth certificate, but his mother had left a letter with his grandfather. The old man never said a word, but the document had been among his things given to the tribal leaders upon his death. An old friend read it to him over the phone. His father had been a high roller at one of the casinos on tribal land. His mother worked there and caught his eye. Eventually they started a relationship. She got pregnant. Eight years later, she left the Reservation to be his wife.

"Of course, I am. Your mother was faithful to me, even before we married. Or are you trying to tell me you know otherwise?" The thought seemed to anger him.

"No."

"Well then, there you are. You're my son. And I'd like to think we could have a good relationship now that we know about each other."

Ghost almost said no again, just to see what the other man would do, but managed to stop himself. Instead, he changed tracks. "Your letter promised legal action if I didn't show. That's not very… fatherly."

"That was before I got to know you. My security team did a little digging. Can't blame a man for wanting to get to know all about a son he suddenly finds out about, can you? And now I know you've served your country well, but you've fallen on hard times. That motorcycle club you're with, well, I'd like to see my son socializing with a better class of people. I can and will help you there."

"No." The word came out fast and emphatic. Shiva's Road MC was his family now. Not this man.

"OK, OK, I can see I'm moving too fast for you. A habit in my business. You don't make money letting grass grow under your feet!"

Donald's business, according to Bytes, barely paid the mortgage on this eyesore these days. Donald's father had been a solid contractor for large scale buildings in downtown Chicago. But cutting corners to underbid other contractors, shoddy supplies, and other poor trade practices had given the family business a bad name. Donald scrambled to cover his monthly debts and if he didn't hire better lawyers, he'd be facing jail time. Then there was the little matter of his gambling debts...

Instead of replying right away, Ghost let his attention drift around the office. There were business books, decanters containing various kinds of alcohol with the usual glasses, and several framed pictures. One of the pictures caught his eye. Two young women were laughing with their arms around each other in front of a fountain. One had black hair, dusky skin and a more than passing resemblance to Donald. She must be Rachael, his half-sister.

The other woman -- he didn't recognize her -- was nothing less than stunning. Platinum-blonde hair surrounded her tanned face in a halo as the sunshine poured down on her, seeming to illuminate her from within. The red top she wore hugged her more-than-a-handful breasts and rode up enough to show a strip of her belly. The matching skirt flared out from curvy hips that begged to be gripped with his large hands and held onto for a wild ride. Though he couldn't tell the exact color of her eyes from the photograph, they seemed to sparkle with mischief. And her full lips, painted the same red as her shirt, were a form of temptation all their own. He wanted to lick and suck and taste every inch of her. His cock came to life behind his zipper as he studied the image. He'd never had such a visceral reaction to a woman, let alone one he'd seen only in a picture, in his life.

He shifted in his seat, trying to hide his now hard-as-fuck dick. "Why am I really here?"

Donald sat back in his chair and gave him a shrewd look. "I had hoped we could spend some time getting to know each other before we discussed business, but since you seem eager to get to the point, I'll tell you. Your mother made a foolish decision before her death and I need your help to put things right."

"I'm listening."

"It's just a matter of signing a few papers. We can take care of the matter here, tonight, since you're in such a rush." He slid three pages across the top of his desk toward Ghost.

Bytes' research hadn't turned up a problem with his mother's estate. Really, there wasn't any estate to speak of. She had very little money or property of her own, and all she did have reverted to Donald as her spouse. Only her life insurance policy affected Ghost, and now he understood that detail hadn't been done with dear old Dad's knowledge or permission.

Ghost picked up the papers and quickly scanned them. He saw exactly what his mother had done, and he thought he understood why she had done it, at least in part. Her final wish warmed the heart of the little boy he'd once been. She'd been trying to take care of him in the only way she could.

Donald offered him a pen. "Just sign on the X."

Ghost grinned. "No."

"Son, the cancer... she was in a lot of pain. Heavily medicated. She wasn't in her right mind. Surely you can see she didn't know what she was doing."

"What I see is a man in trouble trying to negate his wife's dying wish."

"Listen to me, son. Your mother never paid one dime of those premiums on that life insurance policy. There wouldn't be any money available if it wasn't for me. That money is rightfully mine!"

"If it was *rightfully* yours, you wouldn't need me to sign these papers," Ghost pointed out.

Donald waved his argument away with a flick of his hand. "A formality. I thought I would save you the trouble and expense of going through the courts, embarrassing the memory of your mother, bringing up her mental state. Lord knows enough doctors were in and out of here who are willing to testify that she wasn't in her right mind when she changed the beneficiary."

Ghost didn't know how his mother had managed to keep this information from Donald, forcing him into this position, but Ghost didn't doubt she'd had a good reason. Ghost wouldn't let her effort be in vain. "Not signing."

"I can see it'll take some time to build up to the trust in me you need to do the right thing here." Donald leaned forward again. His gaze darted briefly to the picture that had captured Ghost's attention a few minutes ago. "Why don't you stay a few days and think it over? Perhaps you'd like to meet your half-sister?"

Ghost had known he had a half-sister, Rachel, a

child from one of his father's mistresses. Seeing the photo of the two young women confirmed Bytes' intel. In the back of his mind, he'd had some vague idea of driving past one of Rachel's classrooms at the University of Chicago to see her, maybe even introduce himself, but he hadn't fully formed a plan. Hanging around the house though... Ghost really had no desire to spend more time in Donald's company than absolutely necessary. Unfortunately, his instinct, the one he trusted to save his ass in the Sandbox on more than one mission, told him to stay with his sperm donor long enough to at least meet Rachel and make sure she was all right. And maybe he would also get a chance to see her friend...

"OK."

* * *

Simone

"How are you doing?" Simone asked her best friend as they sat on deck chairs by the pool, which was illuminated by lights under the water. Night had fallen, and this was as close as they could get to having privacy in this monstrous house.

Rachel tugged the towel tighter around her hips. "Hurts."

Of course she hurt. She'd been raped and beaten by Karl Dupres, the local mob boss who held the bulk of Donald's gambling debts. Simone wished she could take her friend's pain away, but that wasn't how the world worked, at least not here.

She opened her mouth to say something soothing when Donald stepped out onto the balcony attached to his bedroom. He called down to the women to get their attention. "We have guests. I expect you to be welcoming and see to their every need starting tomorrow at breakfast, Simone."

Having made his announcement, he went back inside.

"My turn," Simone mumbled, twisting a lock of her shoulder-length blonde hair through her fingers. What would she be forced to endure this time? Could she do something to work this latest situation to their advantage?

"Don't do anything stupid," Rachel whispered, causing her split lip to bleed again.

"If there's a chance --"

"There won't be. There never is." Rachel got up from her chair with difficulty and stumbled toward the door leading inside.

Simone watched her friend go. Once she was safely inside, Simone let out the breath she'd been holding. There had to be a way out, for both of them. She just had to be smart, wait for the right opening. Even if Rachel had given up hope, Simone hadn't. A solution would present itself. And when it did, she would be ready.

* * *

The following morning, Simone stood outside the solid oak door of the guest suite, fidgeting with her white linen sundress. She now knew who waited for her somewhere on the other side of the door, and her heart pounded inside her chest. Would this man take after his mother or his father? She was prepared, either way.

After taking a calming breath, she knocked on the door. It opened so quickly she was startled into taking a step back. The man now leaning against the frame, seeming not to have a care in the world, had to be Lucas Blackfoot. His inky black hair hung in a wet wave down his back. His black eyes searched her soul.

His dusky bare torso shone as if damp, and his jeans hung off his hips like he'd just thrown them on after getting out of the shower. In other circumstances, she would have found his muscular frame decorated with tribal tats droolworthy. Instead, she had to remind herself she had a task to do. She couldn't afford distractions. Enjoying herself wasn't a priority.

She quickly gathered her wits and pasted a friendly smile on her face. "Hello. My name is Simone. I'm here to escort you and your friend to breakfast."

A second man -- blond, muscular and slightly taller than Lucas -- approached the door and looked over Lucas' shoulder. "Well, you certainly look good enough to eat."

"Beowulf," Lucas said in a warning growl.

"Come on in, pretty girl." Beowulf reached around Lucas to grab her hand and pull her into the suite. "Sit with me while Mr. Grumpy finishes getting dressed."

Lucas continued to glare at his friend, but Simone could only smile at him. When he turned to enter one of the two bedrooms, water from his hair trailed down his back to the curve of his ass and she longed to run her tongue over the trail. Now blushing, and getting a little damp between her legs besides, she quickly sat on the couch next to the grinning blond and tried to think of something benign to say. "So, Beowulf, huh? Were your parents literary buffs?"

The blond laughed. "Beowulf is my road name. Most people just call me Wulf."

"Road name? Like the street you live on?" She wrinkled her nose in confusion.

Wulf laughed even harder. "No, darlin'. We belong to an MC called Shiva's Road. A motorcycle club in Ohio. We all have road names. Names we were given when we patched in. We don't use our birth names. It's a respect thing."

Simone knew next to nothing about motorcycle clubs. Didn't they just ride around in groups on the weekends? Or were they like Hell's Angels, fighting and doing drugs all the time? Neither option made these two good prospects for her true purpose. "So Lucas has a road name?"

"Yup. He's Ghost."

"Why is he called that?" Given how the man's presence affected her, she couldn't imagine how anyone would think of him as a ghost.

"You'd have to ask him. It's his story to tell."

Immediately she tilted her head forward so her hair swung down to cover the renewed blush staining her face. "I'm so sorry. I didn't mean any disrespect."

Lucas -- no, she should call him Ghost -- stepped into the room again. He now wore a tight black T-shirt molded to his muscles, jeans that cupped his balls, and sturdy black boots. Although Wulf had on something similar, Ghost wore the hell out of his clothing.

"I'm ready," Ghost announced quietly.

Simone bounced up out of her seat as if poked by something hot. Could she act any more juvenile? How could she be seen as a seductress at this rate? "Great! If you'll follow me?"

"Sure," Wulf replied.

Ghost made no sound despite his heavy boots as he reached her side. She opened the door to the hall. "Will Rachel be joining us?" Ghost asked, his breath caressing her ear and sending shivers down her spine.

"No, she has other plans this morning, but she's very excited to know you're here." The lie fell easily off her tongue. She hadn't always been good at lying, but current circumstances required her to learn skills schools didn't teach.

"I want to meet her."

"I'll see what I can arrange." She and Wulf kept up an amicable conversation as the trio walked to the morning room off the kitchen. Would Ghost understand the slight? Important guests would be served in the formal dining room. Only family or employees ate here. Even though Ghost was technically family, Donald wanted something from him. The fact that she had been selected to meet them this morning instead of Rachel should also be a red flag to these visitors. Donald was sending a message. Dare she explain it? She wanted Ghost to be forewarned, but at the same time she didn't want to risk making him angry.

"What can I make you for breakfast?" she asked brightly once the guys sat around the white wooden table, still mentally chewing on her dilemma.

"You're going to cook?" Wulf asked. "Don't they have a chef on staff for that?"

"I usually do breakfast for the household. I like to help out." She wiped her sweaty hands down the front of her dress. "So, what'll it be? Pancakes? Omelets? French toast? Eggs Benedict?"

"Coffee. Scrambled eggs. Bacon or sausage. Potatoes of some kind. If it's not too much trouble," Ghost said in his soft, husky voice.

His voice vibrated something deep in her core. She clamped her thighs together and tried to focus on the task at hand. "That's an easy order, Ghost. Are you sure you don't want something more complicated? I assure you I can handle it."

"No, simple is sometimes best."

"OK then. Wulf, what can I make for you?"

He opened his mouth to answer, but Ghost

elbowed him and said, "He'll have the same."

"Coming right up," she answered with a grin.

As she started pulling items out of the refrigerator and putting them on the counter, an idea occurred to her. Although still risky, it would help her sound out the kind of men these visitors were. She began to hum any song she could think of related to heroes. The *Superman* theme. *Hero* by Nickelback. *Holding Out For a Hero* by Bonnie Tyler. Whatever came to mind.

Wulf smiled first and when she paused, he hummed back *We Don't Need Another Hero* by Tina Turner. She thought he got the message, but Ghost surprised her by humming *Rescue Me* with a question in his eyes.

She blinked once, slowly and deliberately, hoping he would understand such an answer. If she nodded, her obvious movement would be caught on camera and be seen by Donald's security goons. As it was, her humming would come under scrutiny.

Just as the thought crossed her mind, the sound of heavy boots hitting the maple floor in the hall reached her ears. Trevor came into view, rounded the counter and stopped next to her. He picked up a piece of cooked bacon she had draining on some paper towels and scarfed it down. "You guys playing some kinda whack *Name That Tune* or what?"

"Just having a little fun while she cooks," Wulf said.

Trevor snagged another piece of bacon, then grabbed her ass with his greasy fingers, ruining her white sundress. "Simone can be a lot of fun under the right circumstances. Can't ya, darlin'?"

She really wanted to hit Trevor in the face with the skillet full of hot grease. She refrained, but like with most things in this house, it was a struggle. "I need to get more bacon from the fridge."

Trevor didn't make it easy, standing in her way so she had to brush against his chest as she turned. Of all the members of the security team in the house, Trevor behaved the worst. He didn't have permission to do more than grope her, but he took advantage of that every chance he got.

As soon as she returned to the stove, Trevor put his hand on her ass. She couldn't help but flinch as he squeezed hard enough to leave fingerprints.

"Remove your hand," Ghost said softly.

Trevor laughed. "Why? Simone here likes the attention."

"Not yours."

"Look here, boy," Trevor said as he moved over to stand beside the table where the other men were sitting. He leaned down and got in Ghost's face. Ghost didn't move back or flinch as the other man continued talking. "I know you think you're all important now 'cause your Daddy is giving you some attention, but Simone knows what the score is, and she likes it. So shut the fuck up and keep your nose out of our business."

"I decide what's my business, not you."

"Listen, you fuck --"

He broke off as a message came through the communicator he wore in his ear. It was a piece of shit device, not shielding the communication at all.

"Trevor, return to base. Now."

Trevor growled. "I'm not done here, boss."

"Did I stutter? Return to base. Immediately."

With a look that promised their conversation was far from over, Trevor stomped his way out of the kitchen.

As soon as he was out of sight, Simone hurried over with food, coffee and all the necessary accessories on a wooden tray. "You shouldn't have interfered," she said softly.

"I should have broken his hand," Ghost replied.

His voice vibrated through her, touching her intimately. She didn't know why he affected her so. He awakened her body in ways she never thought she'd feel, ways she thought she'd be immune to forever. Instead of basking in these new, confusing feelings, she went about setting the table and putting the food in front of the men. "Better eat before the food gets cold."

Author's Note

Many thanks to Marteeka Karland for letting Ghost borrow her ExFil team, including the lovely -- and deadly -- Venus.

More about the Bones MC Multiverse and the members of ExFil:

.changelingpress.com/bones-mc-u-13

Dana Cask

Every book is a mystery to Dana. Whether it's writing one or reading one, she delves into the who, what, when, where and why with a thirst for knowledge. Getting to know the characters and following their journey as it unfolds gives her a thrill she hasn't been able to duplicate in any other activity. She's been known to devour as many as three books in a day, and would write until her fingers bled if her muses allowed.

Although Dana is just getting started on her publishing career, please join her on Facebook and Goodreads, and visit her website often as her MC collection grows to see what Dana has in store for her readers next!

Dana Cask at Changeling Press:
changelingpress.com/dana-cask-a-235

Changeling Press, LLC

ChangelingPress.com

Made in the USA
Columbia, SC
28 June 2024

37702150R00065